Reckless

Other  titles

Reckless

Sue Mayfield

Hodder
Children's
Books

a division of Hodder Headline Limited

For Frank, with love and respect

A Catalogue record for this book is available from
the British Library

ISBN 0 340 85084 1

Typeset by Avon Dataset Ltd, Bidford-on-Avon, Warks

Printed and bound in Great Britain by
Clays Ltd, St Ives plc

The paper and board used in this paperback by Hodder
Children's Books are natural recyclable products made from
wood grown in sustainable forests. The manufacturing processes
conform to the environmental regulations of the country of origin.

Hodder Children's Books
a division of Hodder Headline Limited
338 Euston Road
London NW1 3BH

Acknowledgements

Thanks to Liz Procter – for medical advice (again!),
Frank Mayfield – for BMX info and critical feedback,
and Bob Horne's drama students at Brighouse High
School – for agreeing to role-play scenes from the book.

Also my husband Tim – for his discerning eye, my
agent Elizabeth Roy – for encouragement and support,
and Emily Thomas – for wise and patient editing.

Prologue

Josh opens the car door and steps out on to the pavement. Tucking the shiny silver parcel under his arm he closes the door, smiling nervously at us.

"Go for it!" I whisper. With a look of determination Josh opens the gate and walks slowly towards the house holding the parcel against his chest. He passes a bush with purple flowers and a plastic garden seat. There is a football on the path. Josh kicks it on to the lawn. When he reaches the front door he looks back over his shoulder anxiously and, peering through the car windows, we give him the thumbs up.

"Bless him," says Mum as he reaches for the doorbell.

1

Rachel

Let me tell you about my brother Josh . . .

Josh has always lived dangerously. He likes risk and speed and the thrill of being too high up. I reckon I'm quite daring, but Josh is mental!

I was born first – first by eleven minutes – but Josh walked first, swam first and rode a bike first.

When Josh was six he fell out of a tree and broke *both* his arms. At eight he took a bend too fast and crashed his bike into a brick wall. There's a scar on his forehead like a new moon.

Mum says he once climbed on to the kitchen table to get an orange from the bowl when he'd only just learnt to crawl. That was typical Josh, she says – always in a hurry, no fear of danger.

Josh and Charlie were kindred spirits – peas in a pod. I think what he liked about her most – apart from the fact that she was blonde and gorgeous – was that she was as crazy as he was. She was up for it – up for anything.

We first met Charlie Lewis at Kettlebeck last summer. Kettlebeck is in the Yorkshire Dales. We go there every August and camp in a field beside the river. Kettlebeck is the best place ever. I love it. I love the mates we always meet and the laughs we have. I love waking up in my sleeping bag and feeling the sun on the tent. I love how black the night is without any streetlamps. I love the way the hills turn orange at sunset. And I love the smells – the smell of the woods after rain, the smell of the grass in the morning, the smell of bacon and sausages on all the barbecues.

But most of all I love the river. The river is the best thing about Kettlebeck – or rather the falls are, Kettlebeck Falls. You can hear them from the tent at night, gushing and throbbing over the stones.

Josh was itching to get to the river.

"Hold the pole straight, Joshua," said Dad, "or the awning will be lopsided."

"Can't I just go and check out the water level?" said Josh. "I'll come straight back."

"Oh yeah," said Mum. "If you go to the river you'll be gone hours."

Josh grinned.

"This won't take long," said Dad. 'It'll be up in no time if we all help."

"Can't Rachel hold this?" Josh said.

"I'm pegging guy ropes," I said, waving a mallet above my head.

Mum ducked. "Steady, Rach!" she said.

Dad started singing "Take me to the ri-ver!" Dad's always singing. It's dead embarrassing! "That's the poles secure now," he said, looking pleased with himself. Josh unzipped the awning and stepped outside the tent. I pretended to whack him with the mallet but he pushed me down in the grass and tickled me.

"Are you going off the tree roots?" I asked when he'd stopped.

"Of course!" he said, jumping up.

Charlie was just climbing out of the water when we got to the river. Josh made a soft whistling sound through his teeth when he saw her. She clambered on to a rock, flicking her wet hair out of her eyes. She was wearing shorts and a tight black crop top that clung to her like cellophane. Drips of water ran down her long tanned legs.

She was the only person swimming. A few kids with a dog and fishing nets on bamboo poles were paddling higher upstream but no one else was in the falls. Two girls were sitting on the bank eating a tube of Pringles but they were fully dressed and their hair was dry and neatly gelled. Charlie spoke to them.

"OK," she said. "The big one." The girls watched as Charlie crossed the river, ankle-deep in the shallow water above the falls. Stepping on to the opposite bank she started to scramble up the cliff, picking her way along ledges and grooves in the rock.

There are three waterfalls at Kettlebeck, falling one after the other like stairs. The two top falls are quite small with plunge pools like swirling jacuzzis. The third waterfall is a wide curtain of foam that tumbles into a deep black pool. Cliffs surround the pool like the sides of a basin.

Charlie was high up now, skirting the rim of the pool. Above the cliffs on the far side of the river are woods. One of the trees is right above the pool and its roots reach to the edge making a natural platform. Josh was watching Charlie, cradling his rolled-up towel against his bare chest.

"She's going for the Roots," he said.

For a moment Charlie was hidden in the shade of the enormous tree, then she stepped forward into sunlight. Wedging the toes of her trainers into the grooved roots she steadied herself, looking down at the black water. Reaching up with her hand she hooked her hair behind her ear and fiddled with the strap on her shoulder. Just for a minute it looked as though she'd lost her bottle. Then she jumped – knees bent, hair flailing, plummeting downwards. There was a sharp crack as she hit the water and as she disappeared from view, creamy circles rippled outwards on the surface of the pool. Seconds later her face appeared, smiling and triumphant.

Josh dropped his towel and sprang immediately, pogo-stick straight, into the top pool. Plunging down into the bubbles he bobbed back up, glistening with spray.

He climbed out shaking himself like a wet dog and quickly made his way up the cliff to the line of trees and on to the woody platform. I could tell he was dying to impress the girl in the black crop top – and anyone else that was watching. Joshua loves an audience. He first jumped off the Roots when he was nine. A party of ramblers were going by on the top path and they all stood still and gasped as he jumped. He drew a crowd when he first dived too. That was three summers ago – Josh was twelve then. He's the only person I've ever seen go in headfirst.

Charlie was sitting on the bank now rubbing herself with a towel. Josh was standing ramrod still on the tree roots. He clenched his stomach muscles so you could see his six-pack. Glancing across at the girls on the bank he bent his knees and launched himself off the cliff, swinging his arms above his head like wings and arching into a perfect dive. He entered the water like a torpedo and when he came back up again he had the biggest grin you ever saw.

"He's cute," said one of the Pringles girls.

"He's my brother," I said, basking – not for the first time – in Joshua's glory.

2

Joshua

Charlie was the first girl I ever saw go off the tree roots. Most of the root jumpers are meatheads – local blokes with tattoos and pierced eyebrows that come on hot days and jump in in their clothes. Loads of people swim at Kettlebeck in the summer. Some of them just go in the top pools, or in the shallow bits higher upstream, but the black pool is best. There are four places you can jump from. There's the Step, a rock at the side of the biggest waterfall that you can stand on – provided the river level isn't too high. Jumping off there it's a six-foot drop to the water. Then there's the Overhang – that juts out about twelve feet above the pool. People run along it and bomb off the top. At the top of the cliff on the other side there's the Ledge, a little shelf of rock about fifteen feet high. That gets slippery when lots of people have been jumping in so you have to be careful. Then, twenty feet up, there's the Roots. To get out of the pool again you either have to scramble up the falls on to the Step or you can swim downstream where there's a rusty iron ladder fastened to the cliff.

* * *

We've been going to Kettlebeck since I was five. The first time I jumped off the Step Dad was in the water waiting to catch me. The cold punched the breath out of me. It still does, with the first few jumps, only now I'm more used to it.

Rachel thinks I jump in to show off, but I don't. I do it for me. It's the most amazing feeling. All winter long I dream about doing it.

After the first jump I went and wrapped myself in the towel. The girl in the black top was back in the water by then. She was standing under the waterfall in the top pool so that the water cascaded over her head and shoulders. She was seriously nice-looking – lovely face, luscious lips, masses of crinkly hair. She was in great shape too. I noticed she had a tiny sparkly stud in her navel.

Two other girls were watching her, stuffing their faces with crisps. I thought they were all together so I walked over and said, "What's your friend's name?" They looked at each other and smirked, then one of them said, "She's not our friend." There was a pause and then the other girl said, "She was already here when we arrived."

"D'you want a crisp?" said the first girl, leaning towards me with a tube of Pringles.

"Cheers" I said, taking one.

"What's your sister called?" she said, nodding

towards Rachel. Rachel was floating on her back in the middle pool. "Rachel," I said.

"You're dead alike," the other girl said.

"We're twins," I said.

"Ah that's nice," said the girl with the Pringles, twiddling her hair.

I let the towel fall off my shoulders and felt the warm sun on my back. The goosebumps on my arms had just about gone.

"What's your name?" one of them said.

"Josh," I said, running my fingers through my hair.

"I'm Katie," she said, "and this is Kelly."

"Hi!" I did a cheesy wave but I wasn't really listening. The girl in the black top was getting out of the water and heading for the trees again. Her body was a lovely curvy shape in her wet clothes. She glanced across the river and caught my eye and then looked away. I dropped my towel in the grass and jumped into the top pool. By the time I surfaced the girl had reached the Roots. This time she didn't hesitate but leapt right out into the middle of the pool. As she climbed out on to the Step I dived off the Overhang. She was sitting on the waterfall when I emerged again. Fountains of water were spraying up on either side of her. She was clapping.

"Nice dive!" she said.

"Thanks," I said. I climbed out and sat on a rock.

"Was that your first time off the Roots?" I asked.

"Yep," she said. "We've been here all week – I've been working up to it!" She laughed and shook her hair.

"Awesome isn't it?" I said. I was shivering with cold. I wrapped my arms across my chest.

Just then a kid came running along the bank. He was shouting but the noise of the river drowned out what he said. He came a bit nearer and shouted again.

"Charlie!" he yelled. "Charlie!" I could just make it out.

The girl looked round and then pulled a face.

"Is he shouting to you?" I asked.

" 'Fraid so," she said.

"Charlie, Mum says you've got to come now. We're going to the shops." The kid was hopping about on the bank.

"My little brother," she said, pulling another face. "Great!" She stood up and waded out of the river.

Picking up her towel she set off across the field.

"Charlie!" I shouted after her. She turned round, surprised. "See you again," I said. She smiled.

"See you!" she shouted back, and she disappeared through the gap in the hedge.

3

Rachel

The next day was hot, very hot. Lots of kids came to the river. One of them was Harry. Harry had thick black hair and a string of beads on a leather thong – and a wet suit! No one wears wet suits at Kettlebeck. He also had a rubber dinghy. He was holding it slung across his back like a tortoise's shell.

"Throw it in," said Josh.

Harry laughed. "Oh yeah!" he said.

"I'm serious," Josh said. "Throw it off the Overhang then you can jump in and swim to it."

Harry looked nervously down at the dark pool. The water at Kettlebeck is stained brown with peat, like cold tea.

"Is it deep?" he asked. He put two plastic oars down on the ground.

"Twenty feet or so," Josh said. Harry looked doubtful.

"It's OK though," Josh said. "There aren't any rocks poking up. It's very safe."

"What about the current?" said Harry. I liked his voice – the way he said the double r sound in current.

"It isn't very strong in the pool and the river's

moving quite slowly by the time you get down to those rocks. There's a ladder just round the bend where you can scramble out again," Josh said, pointing downstream.

Harry didn't look convinced. "Is it cold?" he said.

"Not in *that* thing!" said Josh. He gestured to Harry's wet suit with a grin. Harry didn't react. He was peering over the rocky ledge at the foaming water.

"You do it," he said to Josh, swinging the boat off his shoulders. Josh jumped at the invitation. (We had a dinghy last year but it burst when Josh and four of his mates jumped into it all at once.)

Harry dropped the orange dinghy over the edge so that it landed at the bottom of the biggest waterfall. The current caught it and carried it a few metres out. It spun a little in the swirling water. Straight away Josh jumped off the Overhang and swam to the dinghy. He slithered into it like a slippery fish. Harry was clapping on the cliff above.

"Here," he shouted. Picking up one of the oars he threw it into the pool. Josh fished it out of the water and paddled himself, canoe style, downstream a little.

"Smart!" said Harry as Josh came running back along the bank, carrying the dinghy on his head like a giant sombrero.

Josh threw the boat in a second time.

"Go on," he said to Harry.

"Nah," Harry said. "You go."

Josh jumped again. This time he landed smack on the boat making it bob and splash. I threw an oar to him. Josh was grinning up at us from the wet boat.

"Come on in, the water's lovely!" he said.

"Go on," I said and I jumped. To my surprise Harry jumped too. We came up within a few metres of each other and swam towards the dinghy. Josh grabbed my hand and hauled me in then we both grabbed Harry. He flopped heavily into the boat, looking like a seal in his shiny wet suit.

"Well done," said Josh.

"God! It's cold!" said Harry.

"You soft sod!" Josh said.

It was a squash with all three of us in the boat.

"Is this meant to be a *three* man boat?" I asked.

"I doubt it," said Harry, "but you're definitely not a man so that's OK. I'm Harry by the way."

"Hi Harry!" we both said and then Josh said, "Ta for the use of the boat." Harry smiled. He had lovely twinkly eyes.

When we got back to the top of the waterfall Charlie was there, standing on the Overhang, ready to jump. As we watched she sprang into the black pool, pointing her toes like a gymnast.

"Your turn," said Josh, handing Harry the dinghy rope.

"You go," Harry said. "It's a bit cold for me."

Josh hurled the dinghy off the cliff and plunged in after it. By then Charlie was in the middle of the pool treading water. Josh got into the dinghy.

"Can I have an oar?" he shouted. Harry threw an oar but it was a bad throw and it landed right on the other side of the pool.

"Oops!" said Harry. "Soz!" Josh started to paddle using his hands but he didn't get very far.

Charlie laughed and started doing front crawl towards the oar. She reached it in no time and holding the oar above her head she said to Josh, "Do you want this?"

"Thanks," he said. I saw him reach out for it but Charlie snatched it away from him.

"What's it worth?" she said, laughing.

"A free boat ride?" said Josh.

"It's a deal," said Charlie. Charlie climbed into the boat and sat behind Josh with her long brown legs dangling over the sides. It may have been sunburn but Josh's face suddenly looked very red.

"I dare you to go over the waterfall," Charlie said.

"In the dinghy?" said Josh.

"Mad!" said Harry.

We were sitting on the grass above the falls. Charlie

tossed her hair back over her shoulders. It had dried out now. It gleamed in the sun. I trailed my toes in the water.

"Who's up for it?" Charlie asked.

"Are you serious?" said Josh.

Charlie stood up. Josh was looking at her, amazed. "Come on!" she said.

"What if you burst the dinghy?" I said.

"Don't be boring, Rachel," Josh said.

"It's not our dinghy Josh, it's Harry's," I said, giving him a look. Harry was smiling.

"Go for it!" he said. "But you're mental!"

Charlie waded into the shallow water above the falls, towing the dinghy behind her.

"Help me," she said. Josh followed her.

"You hold it while I get in," she said. She handed the rope to Josh.

"She's crazy," said Harry. He was smiling delightedly. People further up the bank had stopped to watch.

Josh held the sides of the boat while Charlie got in. The current was pulling powerfully at the flimsy boat but as soon as Charlie's weight was in the dinghy it rested on the rocky riverbed and wouldn't budge.

"You can let go now," said Charlie.

"I have let go," said Josh. "The water's too shallow!"

"Give her a push!" Harry shouted.

"Careful!" said a man with a black dog.

Josh gave the dinghy a shove and the water lifted it and carried it right to the edge of the falls. But then it stuck again.

Charlie rocked her body vigorously like a child trying to make a rocking horse go. Nothing happened. She rocked again.

"Ride 'em cowboy!" Harry shouted. Suddenly the boat slid forward and its nose tipped downwards over the falls.

"Here I go!" said Charlie. She gave one more rock and the dinghy was plummeting down, hanging almost vertical in the curtain of water. Charlie gripped the sides of the boat. Her hair flew out all around her face like a ring of fire.

"Oh – my – God!" she yelled as she slid down the falls. We all ran to the edge and peered into the black pool. Charlie had disappeared. The dinghy had flipped over and was sitting on the water like a big orange mushroom. Charlie was nowhere to be seen. No one spoke. Josh was standing stock still at the top of the falls looking into the bottomless water. Still Charlie didn't appear.

"Go and get her!" I said to Josh. "She might have banged her head."

Josh was about to dive. His face was white with panic. The man with the black dog was running along the bank. Just then Charlie's head appeared in the pool, a few metres from the overturned dinghy. Her eyes were closed and she was gasping for breath.

"Oh God," I said. I thought she was drowning.

Then she opened her eyes, shook her head and laughed. "Scared you!" she said. She swam to the boat, flipped it right way up and clambered in. Without saying a word Josh dived off the falls and disappeared underwater. A few seconds later Charlie screamed. The boat was lifting up out of the water with her sitting in it. It was tipping sideways, rolling over as if a huge whale had swum underneath it. The whale was Josh. His head and shoulders emerged under the boat. With a jerk he pushed Charlie right out into the pool. As she bobbed back to the surface Josh splashed her wildly.

"You had us all scared!" he said. "You daft nutter!"

4

Joshua

We found the rope swing that afternoon. I rowed downriver in the dinghy with Charlie. Rachel and Harry walked along the bank. Harry had taken his wet suit off by then, thank goodness. He looked a right wally in it! And anyway it was a roasting day.

The Pringles girls followed us too – downstream past a load of sheep and a field with horses in it.

Charlie was trailing her hand in the water trying to catch fish.

"There's one!" she yelled. "Damn! I nearly got it! I was *that* close." She held up her thumb and forefinger with a tiny gap between them. "Row faster!" she said.

The rope swing was just past the bridge, dangling from a tree right over the river. The river is much more shallow there than at the falls but there's a deep patch right in the middle. I went first on the swing. It was a blue nylon rope – pretty thick and strong. Someone had tied a wooden pole like half a broom handle on to the end of it like a trapeze. There was a fork in the tree where you could stand to launch off. I jumped, and hooking my legs over the pole I swung out across the water and back again.

"Cool!" I said.

"Drop into the water!" Charlie shouted. "I dare you!"

So I swung again. This time I held the pole in both hands like a zip line and pushed off hard from the tree. When I was as far out as I could get, I let go and fell into the river with a huge splash.

"Is it deep?" Rachel asked. I could just touch the riverbed with my feet.

"Neck deep," I said.

Charlie was in the tree and holding the rope before I was even out of the water. She swung out, pedalling her legs as if she was on an invisible bike, and dropped into the river with a Tarzan-like yell.

We stayed there all afternoon. Falling into the cool river on such a hot day was a fantastic feeling. Charlie got more and more mad, jumping from higher and higher up the tree and doing star jumps and turns in the air above the water. Rachel says *I'm* a show-off but Charlie was well worse!

Rachel jumped in too and even Harry had a go – *without* his wet suit.

"Mind you don't catch cold," I said. Harry laughed.

Katie and Kelly kept well away from the water. They sat on a rock with their jeans rolled up, trying to tan their legs and eating a big bag of M&Ms. Every now and then they threw me one and I caught it in my mouth like a performing sea lion.

* * *

We had to carry the dinghy back as the current was too strong to row against. Mum and Dad were cooking a barbecue. The field was full of smoke and gorgeous smells.

"Do your mates want some food?" Dad said. "Mum bought about ninety chicken legs!"

"They were on special offer," said Mum indignantly.

I looked at Charlie. "Yeah, cool," she said. "Thanks."

Harry stayed too. I reckon Rach fancied him because she went off to the toilet block and came back with make-up on and her most revealing top. "Going somewhere special, Rach?" I said and she shot me a look.

Dad was singing "Don't worry, be happy!" as he speared the chicken legs with a long fork. "Embarrassing!" said Rachel, looking cross. Then Harry joined in singing. He's a weird kid!

When we'd all stuffed ourselves big style and were lying in the grass, Dad suggested a game of rounders. He marked out the bases with camping chairs and started practising his bowling against the side of the tent.

"I'll play," said Harry.

"OK," said Rachel. "You and me against Charlie and Josh."

"What about me?" said Mum, pretending to be hurt.

"You can be with us, Mum," I said. Just then Charlie's little brother appeared.

"Can I play?" he said. Charlie groaned.

"You can be with *us*. I hope you're good," said Rachel. "What's your name?"

"Dominic," said Charlie, "and he's rubbish!"

Dominic stuck his tongue out at Charlie. I spotted Katie and Kelly a few tents away. Katie was talking on her mobile.

"Come and play rounders," I said. "We need more players."

"I hate rounders," said Kelly, but they came anyway.

Katie was on our side. She was useless. Her mobile rang when she was halfway between second and third base and she stopped running! Mum was good though. She hit the ball for miles.

"Well in Mum!" I shouted as she sprinted for fourth base.

And Charlie was stunning. She ran like the wind. We won by seventeen rounders.

I took me ages to get to sleep that night. It was hot and sticky in the tent and Rach was snoring. In my head I was falling from the rope swing over and over again – falling into the ice-cold Guinness-coloured water – falling and falling again. And every time I surfaced Charlie was there, smiling at me, with beads of river water coursing down her face.

5

Rachel

We'd been at Kettlebeck a couple of days when Danny and Dig arrived. Danny was into football in a big way and Dig had a stunt bike. They were camping with their dad who was called Jez and was very tall with a long black ponytail. They pitched their tent in the spot right next to ours.

"Nice bike," said Josh. It was a silver BMX. Dig was doing wheelies and bunny hops in front of our tent. Danny was playing keepie-uppie with a football.

"There are some good bumps and ramps in the field by the river," Josh said, "if you're into dirt jumping that is ..."

"Cheers," said Dig.

We went down for a swim after lunch when the sun had moved round on to the black pool. Harry was there and Charlie and Charlie's dog Marge. Charlie threw a stick for Marge, upriver where the water's only waist deep. Marge plunged in and swam after it. When she came out she shook herself all over the blanket we were sitting on.

"Mar-ge!" shrieked Charlie, who was lying face

down in the sun. Marge flopped on to the grass panting. Her damp fur was sticking out in tufts.

"Great hair-do," I said, laughing at her.

We hadn't been by the river long when Dig appeared on his bike. He started zipping backwards and forwards across the field, jumping ramps and doing stunts – granny airs and table-tops and things (I can never remember which one is which). Josh got out of the river where he'd been swimming and pulled on his clothes and shoes.

"Can I have a go?" I heard him say to Dig. The next thing I knew Josh was on Dig's bike leaping across ditches and rocky bumps, going through his whole repertoire of tricks. Charlie rolled over on to her side so she could see him. She looked impressed.

"Has he done this before?" she said, as Josh sailed through the air.

"He does it all the time at home," I said. "Him and his mate Jamie. They go off on their bikes with spades and dig trenches to jump over – out on the moors."

"Cool," said Charlie.

She took a bottle of suntan lotion out of her bag and rubbed some on her legs. I noticed the thud thud thud sound of a football bouncing off someone's knees. It was Danny. He was still doing keepie-uppie, counting under his breath, "thirty-nine, forty, forty-one . . ."

I took some nail varnish out of my bag and started painting the nails on my left hand. I did one nail blue, one green, one purple, one pink and one orange then, when that was dry, I painted spots and stripes on them.

"Will you do mine too?" Charlie said, stretching out her long brown fingers towards me on the blanket.

"What colour?" I said.

"Purple and green stripes," she said. Carefully I started painting purple stripes down the middle of each nail. Charlie was watching Josh further down the field.

"Has Josh got a girlfriend?" she said.

"No," I answered. "Why? Are you interested?" I asked.

"Maybe," said Charlie. "He's fun. I like him." Right on cue Josh shouted across to us and waved.

"Bit of a poser though," Charlie said with a grin.

"Tell me about it!" I said.

"He's nice-looking," Charlie said.

"He's a babe magnet!" I said with a laugh. Josh is pretty good-looking. He's good fun too. And kind. And caring. And clever. And funny. But then he is my twin!

The thudding of Danny's football was getting louder and louder. I could hear his voice keeping the score.

"Seventy, seventy-one, seventy-two, seventy— Oh shit!" The thudding stopped.

"Great," said Charlie quietly. "He's dropped it. The noise was starting to get on my nerves." I smiled. Danny was picking his ball up off the ground.

"He's off again," I said.

"One, two, three . . ." said Danny. Thud thud thud went his knees on the ball.

I'd finished Charlie's nails. She blew on them to dry the polish. My pots of colours were spread in a row across the blanket.

"Who's next?" I said, looking around the field.

Marge was lolling in the grass beside us. Her grey fur was dry and fluffy again now. "Paint Marge's toenails," Charlie said. "She could do with a bit of a make-over!"

I'd never painted a dog's toenails before but there's a first time for everything. She struggled a bit so it was pretty messy. I gave her purple claws on one of her front paws, green on the other and was halfway through painting orange claws on one of her back paws when she got fed up and wandered off into the shade.

"Come back Marge," said Charlie. "You look beautiful!"

Just then Harry climbed out of the jacuzzi pool where he'd been swimming and wrapped himself in a towel.

"Harry's nice," I said.

"He's bit chubby," said Charlie. She was looking at Josh who was walking towards us with his shirt off.

Dig had got his bike back at last.

"That was wicked!" Josh said. "Did you see my one handed X-Up?"

" 'Fraid not," I said. "Do you like Marge's toenails?"

Josh pulled a bottle of Coke out of the bag and took a long swig.

Thud thud thud went Danny's football. "Twenty-five, twenty-six, twenty-seven, twenty-eight . . ."

Suddenly Charlie jumped up off the blanket and ran towards Danny. He looked startled as she snatched his ball and dodged out of his way.

"Oi!" he shouted. "What the heck?"

"Sorry, mate," Charlie said, "you were being annoying!" She threw the football into the river just above the top waterfall. We watched, amazed, as it splashed into the swirling pool. Catching the current it bobbed and spun before careering down the second waterfall into the next pool.

"Send Marge after it!" I said.

"Get it, Marge! Fetch!" Charlie shouted, laughing. Marge ran along the bank barking excitedly.

"Get it!" shouted Danny. "That cost me ten quid!" The ball was spinning in the second pool, inching nearer and nearer to the waterfall.

"Fetch, Marge!" Charlie shouted. Marge barked again, wagging her tail furiously. She had no intention of swimming.

"Useless dog," said Charlie as the football lurched over the edge and plummeted into the black pool.

"Get my ball back quick you stupid cow!" Danny yelled as he hopped about on the bank.

"OK, keep your hair on," Charlie said. She was pulling off her shoes, ready to swim.

Suddenly there was a huge splash. We peered over the rocky overhang into the frothing pool. There was Josh still wearing all his clothes, bobbing in the black water. He swam towards the football and grabbed it in one hand.

"Got it," he said, smiling.

On the top of the cliff Charlie struck a pose like an old movie star, hands clasped together, eyelids fluttering.

"My hero," she said in a silly voice. Everyone laughed, even Danny.

6

Rachel

I love night-times at Kettlebeck. I love the way it gradually gets dark and the warmth and colour leak out of the sky and hills until everything is black and white and cool.

The first night Danny and Dig were there we all ended up in the field by the river. Charlie brought her blanket and wrapped herself in it. Harry had a box of Jaffa Cakes. Katie and Kelly had a big bag of Doritos with a jar of cheesy dip. It was Dig's idea to play dares.

"Spin the bottle," he said, throwing an empty Coke bottle down in the grass.

Josh was sitting on a rock that gleamed like silver in the moonlight.

"I'll spin," he said.

He spun the bottle. It stopped with its top pointing at Harry.

"Wahey!" said Josh. "A dare for Harry . . ."

"Make it an easy one!" Harry said, pulling the hood of his fleece over his ears.

"Sing a nursery rhyme," Josh said.

Harry stood up and cleared his throat. "No sweat,"

he said. He sang Humpty Dumpty without batting an eyelid. Everyone clapped when he'd finished.

Dig was next. Danny dared him to eat some grass. Dig pulled up a couple of blades and put them tentatively to his lips.

"Down in one! Down in one!" Josh chanted. Others joined in. Kelly shone her torch on Dig's mouth.

"Chew and swallow," she said. Dig put the grass in his mouth and sucked it a bit. Then he spat it out.

"Yuck!" he said. "It tastes like sheep shit!"

I spun the bottle and it pointed to Katie.

"Eat some sheep shit!" said Danny with a grin.

"No way!" she said.

"It's my turn to choose the dare," I said. I knew it wasn't worth giving Katie anything too taxing or she'd just wimp out and get the giggles, so I dared her to stuff her mouth with Doritos and then tell a joke. Even that made her so giggly nobody could understand the joke.

Kelly dared Danny to wear her lipstick. I shone the torch on him while she daubed it all over his mouth.

"You look tasty, Danny," Harry said in a high voice. "Do you want to come back to *my* tent?" Danny laughed. He seemed to have got over losing his football.

Josh dared Dig to go back to the campsite, stand outside someone's tent and growl. We all followed him and peered through the hedge to watch him do it. He chose a tent that was all in darkness and creeping up behind it he did this amazing throaty growl. Then he turned round and legged it back to the field. A few seconds later we heard voices and the sound of a zip then a torch shone over the hedge.

"Sssh!" said Danny. "No one speak!" We crouched low in the grass. The circle of light from the torch scanned the field. I could hear Josh spluttering, trying not to laugh. After a moment the torch light went away and we heard a man's voice say, "It's just kids, I think – little buggers!"

Charlie spun the bottle and it pointed to me. She grinned at me from inside her blanket.

"Rachel," she said. "I dare you to snog ..." She paused. I knew what she was going to say. My stomach gave a lurch. ". . . Harry," she said.

Josh cheered.

"Go for it Rach!" he said. Harry was nibbling chocolate off a Jaffa Cake. I could see his teeth and the whites of his eyes glowing in the dark.

"Rach-el! Rach-el!" Josh chanted. Danny and Dig joined in.

"Come on then!" Harry said. "I'm not *that* bad."

I stood up and walked across to where he was sitting. Kelly shone her torch on us. I kissed him on the lips. He tasted of chocolate. I was glad it was dark and no one could see me blushing.

Somewhere down by the river an owl hooted. Then Kelly spun the bottle and it pointed to Josh. Kelly went all giggly. "I can't think of one," she said.

"I've got one," Charlie said. She poked her leg out from under the blanket and, pulling off her sandal, she dipped her toe in the pot of cheese dip.

"Josh," she said, holding her foot up to him, "I dare you to lick the cheesy dip off my toes!" I happen to know that Josh hates blue cheese dip. But all the same he licked Charlie's toes.

"Gross!" said Harry, eating another Jaffa Cake.

When Dig spun the bottle it landed on Josh again. "I know!" Dig said. "You were mad enough to go in the river this afternoon with all your clothes *on* . . . so I dare you to go in *now*, with *no* clothes on!"

"Good one!" said Danny.

"As if?" said Katie, tipping the last of the Doritos into her mouth. I looked at Josh. I wasn't sure he'd do it. Even Josh has his limits.

"Are you up for it Joshua baby?" Harry said in an American accent.

Josh stood up and walked towards the river. The sound of it swirling and gushing seemed louder in the darkness. The foamy torrents glowed like threads of pearls. Josh silently took off his jeans and his trainers. He pulled his jumper and T-shirt over his head. There he was, standing in his boxer shorts, facing the black river.

"*No* clothes, Josh," Dig said. In one quick movement Josh whipped off his boxers and jumped off the Overhang. All we saw was a flash of his bum like a full moon.

"Meathead!" said Danny.

"God it's cold at night!" came Josh's voice from the pool below. I could see his arms like white propeller blades in the water.

"Quick!" said Harry. "Hide his clothes." We all grabbed Josh's things and ran up the field towards the campsite.

"That's dead tight!" said Katie as she trotted through the damp grass.

"Let's hide up at the toilets," Harry said. "In the park."

We went through the gate in the hedge, running silently between tents and caravans towards the light of the toilet block. I looked back. Josh was running across the field – a streak of white flesh in the darkness.

We piled into the adventure playground beside the toilet building. Dig climbed on to the top of the climbing frame. From there you can see the whole campsite.

"There he is," said Dig pointing. "Look!" I scrambled up the cargo net on to the top. Josh was dodging about the campsite stark naked, weaving in and out of people's tents.

"He's coming this way," said Danny, snorting with laughter.

Just then I heard Mum's voice.

"Josh?" she said, "What's going on?" I saw a torch beam flash and then I heard Mum and Dad howling with laughter. They sounded as if they were going to burst. Then, over the top of their laughing we heard Josh say, "Bastards took my clothes!"

7

Rachel

It rained that night. The next morning the hills were hidden in mist and there was a big puddle outside the tent. The river was raging – fast and creamy and too dangerous to swim in.

"You'll have to think of something else to do today," Mum said as she fried bacon under the dripping awning. "It'll take the river a day or two to settle again. It must have rained really hard."

"It's Josh's fault for doing his naked rain dance," said Dad with a smirk.

Josh grunted from inside his sleeping bag.

"Do you fancy some cheesy dip for breakfast?" I said. Dad was singing, "But it's raining . . . raining in my heart . . .!"

It was my idea to go for a walk. It had stopped raining by the middle of the morning. There were even some patches of blue sky – like holes in a grey curtain.

Charlie brought Marge. Dig and Danny brought a frisbee. Harry brought his brand new shiny green wellies.

"Wow!" Josh said. "You've really got the gear, haven't you Harry?"

Harry smiled at me and I remembered the chocolatey kiss.

Josh wanted to boulder hop, lower downstream where the river narrows and there are loads of rocks. We jumped from rock to rock out into the middle of the stream, following Josh in a line like Follow-my-leader. Some of the rocks were close enough together to walk from one to another like stepping stones. Some you had to take a run up and jump across the gap. Some you had to scramble a bit and use your hands to grab hold. One or two rocks were slippery from the splashing of the river. Danny slipped on one and got his trainers soaked. "Unlucky!" Dig said, leaping past him.

Marge had the right idea. She stayed on the bank, running alongside us and barking like an army drill instructor giving us orders.

"Shut up Marge!" Charlie shouted.

I was fine until we reached a gap between two big slippery boulders that was wider than my legs. The rock furthest away from me sloped upwards like a steel roller-blading ramp. Water was funnelling between the two rocks, spurting up in an arching fountain.

"Now what?" said Harry. "We jump!" said Josh. Josh jumped first and cleared the gap, landing on the far rock on all fours and pulling himself up its sloping face with his hands. Dig jumped next and he cleared the gap too. Charlie braced herself ready to jump. She was wearing shorts and a baggy jumper.

"You could just wade across," I said. Charlie's legs are so long that I bet she could have walked across without getting her shorts wet.

"I'll jump," she said. She took a running leap and hurled herself across the water. Josh grabbed her arm as she landed on the rock.

"Pull me up! I'm slipping!" she said. Josh pulled her arm and she scrambled up the sloping rock face, falling against Josh as she stood up. Josh wrapped his arms across her back to steady her. He kept his arms there for much longer than he needed to.

I jumped next and only just made it. My foot slipped as I landed and I lost my balance and wobbled. Grabbing the rock with one hand I shouted, "Help me!"

Josh and Charlie were standing with their shoulders touching. Josh was gazing at Charlie. He didn't seem to hear me shout. Dig grabbed my other hand and hauled me clear of the water but I skinned my knee on the rock.

"Thanks a bunch, Josh," I said crossly. "Thanks for helping."

I sat down on the rock and rubbed spit on to my grazed knee. It stung like mad. Danny jumped across and landed right by me. Now only Harry was left on the far side of the spurting water.

"I think I'll go back," he said. "I'll come round the bank and meet you. Marge looks like she could do with a bit of company!" He turned round and started stepping back across the stones the way we'd just come.

"Just jump," said Josh. "If you fall in at least you've got your wellies on!"

Harry *did* fall in. He jumped and landed short of the rock. The water was much deeper than his boots – waist deep almost.

"Damn," he said as he clambered out on to the bank. Water was pouring from his trousers.

"Nice one Harry!" said Dig. Harry lay down on his back in the grass and lifted his feet above his head. As he pulled his wellies off river water gushed out of them all over his face. He peeled his socks off and wrung them out with a huge grin. Marge licked the water from his toes. "Ah!" he yelped. "That tickles!"

Just then it started to rain again. It was really heavy rain – big fat plops that splashed against the rocks.

"Run for cover!" I said, scrambling towards the bank.

"I'm soaked already," Harry said, laughing.

Everyone else ran and sheltered under a big tree on the riverbank. Harry sat on the wet grass, pelting rain splattering off his face and hair.

"Strange boy," said Dig, pulling a face. The rain was coming down like bullets, drumming against the broad leaves of the tree. Suddenly a sheet of lightning flashed across the sky. It was followed a few seconds later by a deep rumble of thunder.

"Move!" Harry shouted, waving to us. "Get out from under the tree. You're not supposed to stand under trees in a thunderstorm."

"But it's pouring!" Charlie shouted.

"Why not?" said Danny.

"Why not what?" I said.

"Why shouldn't you stand under a tree in a thunderstorm?" Danny said.

"Something about electricity," said Dig.

"Run!" said Josh. "Into that field. There's a barn – we can shelter in there."

We clambered over the wall into the field. The mud was squelchy and deep. Charlie went up to her ankles in it.

"Can I borrow your wellies?" she said jokingly to Harry.

Calling it a barn was an exaggeration. It *had* been a barn – once upon a time. Now it was virtually a ruin. There were huge holes in the roof where the rain was clattering in. We huddled in one corner, squatting on piles of rocks on the muddy floor.

"There's sheep shit everywhere!" Dig said. "Gross!"

Charlie rummaged in the pocket of her shorts and found a half-eaten tube of wine gums. Peeling it open she started to hand them out.

"One for Rachel," she said as another clap of thunder boomed around the valley. "One for Dig, one for Danny, one for Harry – and one left. You and me will have to share this one, Josh." She smiled at Josh and popped an orange wine gum into her mouth.

"Ten second sucks," she said, counting to ten on her fingers. When ten seconds were up she faced Josh and, planting her lips on his, she passed the wine gum from her mouth to his. A streak of lightning like frayed rope tore across the sky.

8

Joshua

Rachel didn't mention the horse. It was in a field just downstream from the campsite. It was brown with steamy nostrils. Charlie stopped to stroke it on the way to the boulder hopping. She tore a handful of juicy grass from the edge of the riverbank and held it out for the horse, on the flat of her hand. Then Harry produced some Polos from his jeans and gave it those. You could see its huge yellow teeth as it crunched them. Harry patted it and pulled its ears in an expert sort of way.

"Dare you to ride it," said Dig, swinging one leg over the top of the wall as if he was getting on a horse himself.

"No way!" said Harry.

"I will," said Charlie. I thought she was joking.

"Don't you need reins and things?" I asked. My only experience of riding a horse was on the beach at Whitby.

"I'll hold its mane," she said. Before we knew it she'd wrapped her arms around the horse's neck and slid herself off the wall and on to its broad hairy back. Her long legs dangled down the horse's sides.

"Whoah fella, steady now," she purred into its ears.

Harry fed it another Polo and patted its neck. "Is this a good idea, Charlie?" he said. The horse seemed oblivious to the fact that someone was on its back, standing there calmly crunching the sweets.

Then Charlie dug her heels into its sides and made a gentle clicking sound with her tongue. The horse began to walk quietly across the field, away from the river, away from all of us. Charlie gripped its thick mane tightly.

"She's a mad cow," said Danny, shaking his head. I didn't disagree. Charlie Lewis is definitely one mad cow – but she's flipping gorgeous with it.

"Hi ho Silver!" Dig shouted. Charlie lifted one hand and waved.

Everything would have been OK if it hadn't been for the heron. Without any warning a big grey bird lurched upwards from the corner of the field, flying straight in front of the horse and startling it.

"What was that?" Dig said.

"Heron," said Harry. The horse darted sideways and broke into a trot.

"Whoah!" I heard Charlie say, but she had no way of stopping it. The horse got faster and faster. It was galloping now, pounding across the field getting further and further away from us. Charlie was leaning forward, clutching a handful of the horse's mane to keep her balance.

"Whoah!" she said again, louder this time.

In the middle of the field were loads of tall plants – nettles and brambles and spiky purple flowers. The horse swerved to avoid them and Charlie slipped sideways. One of her feet was right up on the horse's back, the other was practically on the ground and she was hanging on tight, her arms across the horse's shoulders, her hair trailing in the mud.

"Help!" she shouted.

I jumped over the wall and ran towards her. The horse had turned and was thundering towards me.

"Help!" she yelled again. As she spoke she let go of the horse's neck and slid to the ground, landing in a clump of nettles.

"Ow!" she yelled.

"Are you all right?" I said, as I drew level with her. Charlie stood up, rubbing her elbow. There was no blood. Amazingly, she looked unharmed. The horse had come to a standstill a few metres away and was eating grass.

I looked at Charlie's arm. Tiny white pimples were appearing on her skin.

"Aagh!" she said. "Nettle stings! Can you kiss it better?"

She held her arm in front of my face and looked straight at me. Without a second thought I kissed her bare arm.

9

Rachel

After the thunderstorm it rained all afternoon and well into the evening. There were streams gushing down the road through the campsite. We all went to the games room. Harry had finally dried out from falling in the river and Charlie seemed to have recovered from falling off the horse. Josh was in a good mood, the sort of mood that makes people feel as if the room is full of sunshine. Charlie was all over him.

The games room at Kettlebeck is smart. It's in a big barn. At one end there are bales of straw and a big tyre swing on a rope from the roof beams. At the other end there's table-tennis, a pool table and a beaten-up old table football game. There's even a vending machine.

Josh went straight to the tyre swing and started swinging like a gibbon.

Charlie stood behind him so she could push the swing. I reckon that was just an excuse to touch Josh's legs! After a bit Josh jumped off on to the straw bales and then he and Charlie started pelting each other with handfuls of straw and rolling about on the barn floor.

It was obvious that night – if it hadn't been already – that Josh and Charlie were heading for big romance. Katie and Kelly looked disappointed. They stuffed their faces with Tootie-Frooties from the vending machine.

Harry was looking really cute in a big white T-shirt. When he challenged me to a game of table-tennis I couldn't refuse. I won by 21 points to 6 which was a bit embarrassing. Every time he missed a point he laughed and apologized. I'm used to playing Josh who usually thrashes me so it was a bit of a walkover.

"Winner stays on," Dig said, taking the bat off Harry and starting to knock up.

Danny appeared and sat on the windowsill level with the net.

"I'll be the ref," he said, tearing the wrapper off a Snickers bar.

"It's umpire," said Dig. "Dummy!"

"I'll be the dummy then," said Danny, "I mean, umpire!" He smiled at me and I laughed.

Josh and Charlie had started a game of pool. Josh seemed to be giving Charlie coaching tips which involved leaning right over her shoulder as she stretched forward with the cue so that their faces were almost touching.

"I think Josh has scored," Dig said as he whacked the ping-pong ball off the table.

"He's welcome to her," Danny said. "She's

bonkers! What was she like on that horse!"

"Nice arse though," Dig said.

"What, Charlie or the horse?" said Harry.

"Shall I go away?" I asked, giving them a disapproving look.

"No, stay!" Danny said. "I want to see you thrash Dig."

"Not literally, I hope," Harry said, pulling the ring-pull off a can of Coke.

"Nice hair too," Dig said, glancing at Charlie who was standing leaning on her cue. She was too far away to hear what he said but, as if sensing the compliment, she tossed her hair back over her shoulder like a shampoo advert.

"I prefer brunettes," said Danny, "like Rachel." I could feel myself blushing.

"I think you're being chatted up, Rachel," said Harry, slurping his Coke.

I sliced the ball over the net but it missed the edge of the table.

"Unlucky!" said Dig. "Let's play." Dig beat me 21–19.

"So close!" said Danny. I gave my bat to Kelly. She giggled and fiddled with her hair. She was pretty useless. Dig won 21 points to 1 and she only scored the point because Dig pretended to drop his bat! Harry was really nice to her.

"Not bad," he said. "You're almost as good as me!"

Dig stayed on and played Danny. I could tell Danny was trying to impress me because he was slamming the ball off the table and giving it lots of spin. Harry handed me his Coke.

"Drink?" he said. His fingers brushed against my hand as I took it from him.

"Cheers!" I said.

"Did you hurt yourself when you fell off that rock?" he said. He said it in a really gentle voice.

"Only a bit," I said. "It's fine now. How about you? Did you hurt yourself when you fell in the river?"

"I've got a bruise on my knee," he said, "and my wellies are a bit soggy, but I think I'll live!"

I handed the Coke back to him.

"Are you as good at table football as you are at table tennis?" Harry asked.

"Nah!" I said. "I'm rubbish!"

"Do you want a game then?" he said, rummaging in his pocket for a 20p coin.

Harry put the coin in the machine and a wooden ball clattered out of a slot.

"Red or blue?" said Harry.

"Can we join you?" It was Josh. "Me and Charlie take you and Rach," he said, taking hold of the blue poles.

"Great," said Harry. "We'll hammer you." He winked at me.

We played three games and Harry and I lost all

three. Then Dig and Danny and Katie and Kelly and Charlie's brother Dominic and a boy with ginger hair all joined in so we were squashed together round the table, five on a team.

Danny positioned himself right by me and kept pressing his elbows against me. I wondered if I should tell him I didn't fancy him but I hate hurting people's feelings.

We were halfway through the game when Charlie's mum walked in. You could tell it was Charlie's mum because she looked like Charlie only older and a bit plumper. She had a purple sundress on and lots of beads. She'd come to get Dominic.

"Bedtime," she said. "It's ten o'clock." Dominic pulled a face.

"Can we finish the game?" he said in a whiny voice.

"OK," said their mum. She sat on the windowsill and lit a cigarette.

"6–3," said Josh, "and four minutes left on the clock."

Charlie glanced up at her mum.

"Mum!" she said. "It's no smoking!" She pointed to a sign on the wall beside the vending machine. Charlie's mum put her finger to her lips and mouthed, "Ssh" with a grin.

The game continued. It was hard to tell who was on which team as everyone was just grabbing at the poles and spinning them wildly. Danny made the noise of the full time whistle. "Game over!" he shouted as the wooden ball clacked down the chute. "Nineteen four to the blues!"

"As if?" said Dig.

Charlie's mum stubbed her cigarette out on the windowsill and dropped the end into the bin.

"OK, Dom," she said.

"What about Charlie? Doesn't she have to come?" Dominic said.

"Not yet," his mum said.

"That's *so* unfair!" Dominic said with a big pout.

"It's not unfair. She's fifteen and you're only ten," his mum said, taking his baseball cap off his head and bopping him affectionately on the forehead with it.

"Come on," she said.

"Night night Dominic," Charlie called as they went out of the door. She blew him a kiss. Dominic turned and silently gave her the finger.

"I love you too Dominic," Charlie said, picking up a table-tennis bat.

It was really dark by the time we left the games room. The rain had finally stopped but all the grass and bushes were glistening wet.

I walked back to our tent with Dig and Danny, taking care to give Danny a wide berth in case he decided to grope me. Josh and Charlie peeled off and went towards Charlie's tent at the bottom of the field.

"Night folks," Josh said as he slipped an arm round Charlie's shoulder. Dig and Danny looked at each other and raised their eyebrows.

Josh was ages. When he finally unzipped the tent and crawled in I was nearly asleep. I switched on the torch and shone it in his face. He had a smile so big you could get lost in it.

"Did you ask her out?" I said.

"Don't be nosy!" he said, taking off his T-shirt.

"Tell me!" I said.

"No," said Josh.

"Ve have vays of making you talk!" I said, pointing the torch beam right in his eyes.

"Don't be childish, Rachel," Josh said in a pretend annoyed voice.

I switched off the torch. Josh wriggled into his sleeping bag.

"Did she say yes?" I said.

"None of your business Rachel." I could tell without looking that Josh was grinning all over his face.

"Did you kiss her?" Josh didn't answer, so I hit him over the head with my pillow.

"Twins Josh!" I said. "No secrets." I started tickling him.

"OK, OK," he said, squirming away from me and catching hold of my wrists.

"Yes I asked her out. Yes she said yes. Yes I kissed her." He paused and then he added, "Lots!" I laughed.

"Satisfied?" he asked. I didn't answer. I was wishing Harry had kissed me.

"Sweet dreams Rach," Josh said as if reading my thoughts.

"Sleep well," I said, burrowing down deep in my sleeping bag.

10

Joshua

Rachel's a nosy cow! She thinks just because we're twins that I should tell her everything. I didn't tell her everything though. I didn't tell her just how much I liked Charlie. I didn't tell her how off-my-head in love with her I felt. I didn't tell her how unbelievably sexy kissing her was or how I could hardly sleep from thinking about her.

I was wide awake at seven the next morning so I went for a run along the riverbank – all the way down to the bridge and back on the other side. I must have run four miles or so. I was soaked with sweat when I got back to the tent so I grabbed some clean clothes and went up to the shower block.

When I came back Mum and Rachel were eating Sugar Puffs at the table in the awning and Dad was frying sausages on the gas stove. They all smiled at me and then smiled at each other as if they had some secret they weren't going to tell me. I poured myself some Sugar Puffs.

"Charlie came by," Rachel said grinning. "We said you were off making yourself beautiful."

"Where's the milk?" I said.

"You look lovely," Mum said, handing me a carton of milk.

"Mmm! Smell lovely too," said Dad, turning the sausages.

"We told her to come back in a while," Rachel said.

Dad speared a sausage with a fork and dropped it on to a plate. Dancing across the tent he started singing "Love is all around us . . ."

"Ssh!" said Mum, trying not to laugh. Parents are so childish.

I was on my second bowl of Sugar Puffs when Charlie appeared. She looked wonderful.

"Great smell," she said.

"What? The sausages or Joshua's body spray?" Dad said.

"Don't be embarrassing, Dad," I said.

"I meant the sausages," said Charlie. "But I'm sure Josh smells nice too."

Rachel winked at Mum. I think they thought I couldn't see.

"I was just taking Marge for a walk," Charlie said. "Do you fancy coming?"

"Sure," I said, finishing my Sugar Puffs.

"Would your dog like a sausage?" Dad said. I looked at Marge who was sitting beside Charlie's foot. She was licking her lips.

"Thanks," said Charlie. Dad put the sausage on the grass and Marge sniffed it warily.

"It's probably too hot," Dad said.

"Have a seat," said Mum, pulling up a picnic chair. Charlie smiled.

"Have you been to Kettlebeck before?" Mum asked her.

"No," said Charlie. "It's my first time."

"Do you like it?" Dad said.

"Yeah, it's great," Charlie said. She looked sideways at me and I smiled at her.

"How long are you staying?" Mum said, tidying away the cereal bowls.

"Only till Saturday," Charlie said.

"What day is it today?" I asked.

"Thursday," said Rachel.

"Yeah, only two days left," said Charlie. She caught my eye and I felt a pang in my stomach.

"Oh that's a shame," Mum said, looking at me sympathetically. I looked at Marge. She was gulping down the sausage.

"Where's home?" said Dad, squirting tomato sauce into a bread roll.

"Doncaster," Charlie said.

"Oh that's not far," said Mum. "From us, I mean." She looked meaningfully at Rachel. "An hour maybe."

"Hour and a half," Dad said.

Marge had finished the sausage and was poking her nose into the food box.

"Shall we go?" I said, pulling on a jacket.

"Bye," said Mum as we headed for the river.

"Have fun!" Dad called cheerily. I didn't look back. I didn't want to see their cheesy grins.

11

Rachel

Charlie's last day was red hot. We spent the whole day by the river. Mum and Dad gave us one of those portable barbecues in a foil tray and some burgers. Charlie brought a bowl of salad and a box-load of crisps. We spread blankets and sleeping bags on the grass above the top falls and lay baking in the sun.

"Time to catch some rays," said Josh as he lay spread-eagled across Charlie's rug. Charlie rubbed coconut suntan oil all over his back. If he'd been a cat he would have purred loudly!

Everyone was happy except Marge, who was lying in the shade under a big tree, panting like a steam train. Her tongue lolled out of her mouth like a rasher of bacon. Every now and then she walked into the shallow part of the river and lay down like a hippo in mud, lapping at the cool water.

Harry had a big bottle of Coke and some plastic cups. He was lying, eyes closed, with his head on the upturned dinghy like a giant rubber pillow.

Josh rolled over on his side and moved Charlie's hair off her shoulders with his hand. He was just taking the lid off the suntan oil when Dig arrived on his BMX.

"Here's Dig," I said. Josh didn't react. He poured some oil into the palm of his hand.

"He's got his bike," I said. "And it looks like he's going to jump ramps."

Josh rubbed his hand across Charlie's bare shoulders.

"Aren't you going to join him?" I asked.

"Maybe later," Josh said lazily.

Harry opened his eyes and grinned at me.

"Do you fancy a swim, Rachel?" Harry said. I fancied it. We swam in the top pool under the falls where the water's all whipped and white. If you swim really hard you can go against the flow and get right under the torrents so it pounds down on you.

"Power shower!" said Harry, treading water under the gushing waterfall. I was swimming towards the waterfall. I could feel its spray against my face. Then I let myself go all floppy and the current carried me till I came to rest against the rocky lip and climbed out.

Harry was doing doggy paddle in the middle of the pool. I picked up a stick from the riverbank and threw it into the water.

"Fetch!" I said. Harry swam towards it and took hold of it in his teeth.

"You're a loony," I said laughing. Suddenly there

was a splash and Marge appeared. "You've got competition!" I said. Harry took the stick out of his mouth and threw it for Marge. Then he climbed out and sat beside me on the rock. I could see droplets of water falling off his feet like diamonds. Was this the moment? Was he going to ask me out? I held my breath.

Just then Marge scrambled out of the river and shook herself all over us.

"Cheers, Marge!" said Harry. He stood up. Then he said, "I'm starving. Shall we go and start the barbecue?"

We clambered up the grass and walked barefoot over the springy grass.

Across the field Dig was bike ramping and Danny was playing football with Dominic and Kelly. Josh and Charlie were wrapped around each other on the blanket, kissing. Harry held his finger to his lips. "Ssh!" he whispered. Bending down he picked up one of the plastic cups and ran back to the river. I sat down in the grass and waited. Josh and Charlie hadn't seen me. They looked as if they wouldn't notice if a herd of dinosaurs walked past them.

Harry was coming back carrying the cup very carefully. Drops of water spilled from the rim as he walked. Grinning madly he crept towards the blanket like a pantomime villain and tipped the water all over Josh's back. Josh and Charlie screamed and sat up, shaking themselves. I saw a smile flash across Josh's face. "Bastard!" he said. Harry dropped the cup.

"It wasn't me, it was Rachel!" he said.

"As if?" I said.

"Where's this barbecue?" said Harry. "I'm starving."

"It's in the bag," I said, pointing to a crinkly carrier bag. Harry pulled it out and read the instructions. "Remove all packaging and stand on a flat surface," he said, pulling the cellophane off and sitting the silver tray on the grass.

"Light firelighters ... let flames subside and charcoal burn for 20–25 minutes before commencing cooking ... Oh it's going to be ages before there's food." Harry rubbed his tummy melodramatically.

"Have some crisps," said Charlie, flicking open the box.

"Throw me a bag too," said Josh.

"What flavour?" said Charlie.

"Beef!" said Josh, flexing his muscles.

"Have we got matches?" Harry asked. He rummaged in the carrier bag.

"Oops, minor point," he said. "No matches!"

"I'll go back to the tent," I said, hoping Harry would come too.

"Cheers Rachel," he said, lying down on the blanket. "You're a star!"

"Thanks," I said, feeling peeved.

When I got back to the blanket everyone had gone away. Harry was playing football with Danny and the others and Josh and Charlie were in the river in Harry's dinghy. I lit the firelighters and flames leapt out from under the wire mesh. "Great," I said under my breath. "It looks like I'm cooking the lunch." The burgers were almost cooked by the time Harry came back.

"I need a drink," he said. "It's too hot for football." Danny and Dig crashed down on the sleeping bags and lay like beached starfish.

"Burgers smell good, Rach," Danny said. Harry peeled the clingfilm off the bowl of salad and stuffed four cherry tomatoes into his mouth.

"You look like a teletubby," Dig said, glancing at Harry's puffed-out cheeks.

"Where's Josh?" said Danny.

"In the lurve boat," said Harry.

"The what?" said Katie, sitting down on the rug and rearranging her hair.

"My dinghy," said Harry. "They've disappeared downstream."

"They'll be back soon," I said. "Josh will smell the burgers!"

Just as I said that Josh and Charlie came round the bend in the path, carrying the dinghy between them.

"Weird," said Danny. "You're telepathic, Rachel!"

"It's a twins thing," I said. "I can read his every move."

"What's he going to do next then?" Dig asked, sitting up.

"Help himself to Coke," I said quietly.

Josh lowered the dinghy on to the ground and came towards us.

"Pass the Coke, Harry," he said. Everybody cracked up laughing.

"Nice one!" said Danny.

After we'd finished eating and the charcoal was just balls of white dust I got some coloured thread out of my bag and started making a friendship bracelet. Charlie wanted to make one too. She sat cross-legged on the blanket next to me, took a length of purple thread out of the bag and spread it across her knees.

"Oh, girlie stuff!" said Danny. "More football anyone?"

The others went away – even Josh. That left just Charlie and me.

"This is for Josh," Charlie said, knotting a strand of green thread on to the purple.

"Josh really likes you, you know," I said.

"I like him too," she said, twisting the threads together. "He's lovely."

"Yes," I said. "He is." I wound a piece of red thread round my finger.

Charlie looked at me and smiled.

"You guys are the perfect family," she said.

"How d'you mean?" I said.

"Well, you know," said Charlie, tying a knot. "Mum, Dad, boy, girl – and all really nice and normal."

"Josh isn't normal!" I said. "He's crazy!" Charlie laughed. "And as for Dad . . ." I said.

"He's funny," said Charlie. "I like him."

"Your mum seems pretty sorted," I said.

"Yeah, she's OK," Charlie said. "My dad's a bit of a loser," she said, "but he's off the scene now. I've only seen him twice in three years – thank God."

"Who's that bloke who's with you?" I said. I'd seen a guy with grey hair and shorts playing badminton with Dominic in the adventure playground.

"That's Steve," she said. "He's Mum's new man. He moved in with us about Christmas time."

"What's he like?" I asked.

"He's OK," she said. Then she laughed. "Except he likes country and western music."

"Is he into line dancing too?" I said.

"No," said Charlie "but my gran is. She's got the rhinestone boots and everything!"

"Groovy!" I said.

I'm not sure why I mentioned Sam. I hadn't thought about him in ages. Maybe it was Charlie saying we were a perfect family. Perhaps I wanted to prove we weren't. Maybe I just felt that if I was going to have to share Josh with her she might as well know the secrets too.

"We had another brother," I said. Charlie had a piece of thread between her teeth. She paused and looked at me out of the corner of her eye.

"Younger than us," I said. She didn't say anything.

"He died when he was three," I said. "He'd have been Dominic's age now."

"What happened?" Charlie said.

"Mum had a car crash," I said.

"God," said Charlie. "Sorry."

Out of nowhere I felt as if I was going to cry. Josh saved me. He came running across the field.

"Here comes Josh," I said, cutting a blue thread with a decisive snap of the scissors.

Charlie tied the bracelet she'd made on to Josh's wrist. It was purple and green – the same as the stripes I'd painted on her nails.

"You've got to wear it for ever," she said. Josh smiled.

"For ever?" he said, raising his eyebrows.

"Promise me you'll never take it off," Charlie said.

"I promise," he said, and he kissed her.

12

Rachel

We had a fire on Charlie's last night, on a shingly beach just downstream from the falls. We collected sticks and built a wigwam out of them. Marge thought it was a game and kept grabbing on to the sticks with her teeth!

"We've got matches this time," I said, fishing the matchbox from lunchtime out of the pocket of my shorts.

The fire was surprisingly successful. Harry had a bag of marshmallows. He poked them on to the ends of twigs and pressed them close to the flames to toast them. The only bad thing was the midges. There were clouds of them swarming round our heads and biting us. Dig had a big bracken leaf that he kept whacking his arms with.

"I know what we need," Charlie said. She ran off up the path.

"Where's she gone?" Dig said. "God knows," said Danny.

Charlie came back with a packet of cigarettes and a twelve pack of Stella Artois.

"I went for these," she said, holding up the

cigarettes. "If we smoke it'll keep the flies off."

"And the beers?" said Harry hopefully.

"They were in the tent. I thought Mum and Steve wouldn't miss them."

"Smart!" said Dig.

"Have we got a bottle opener?" said Harry.

"Shit," said Charlie. She lit a cigarette in the fire.

"My turn," said Josh, standing up. "I'll go and get ours."

Josh came back with a tin opener, a blanket, and a bag of fun-size Mars Bars.

"Oh yes!" said Harry delightedly. I thought of the chocolatey kiss and wondered if another one might be on the cards. The fire crackled and popped. Silver smoke curled upwards.

Josh lit a cigarette. He tried to make it look like he'd smoked before. Mum would have gone mental if she'd seen him. But the midges went away.

Dig tried to get a game of dares going but no one seemed in the mood. Josh was unusually quiet. He sat with his arms round Charlie stroking her hair and kissing her shoulders. He looked like he'd fallen for her big time.

When the beer was all drunk and the fire was just glowing embers Charlie and Josh said something unconvincing about taking Marge for a walk and went off down the riverbank hand in hand.

"He's going to be a miserable bunny tomorrow

when she leaves," Harry said, spinning his empty beer bottle in the grass.

"It's gone chilly," I said, rubbing my arms and shivering. I was hoping Harry might put his arm round me but instead Danny said, "Come under the blanket if you like Rachel."

"No I'm fine thanks," I said, shuffling closer to Harry. We sat there for ages, talking about nothing. Then Marge appeared – her eyes shining in the moonlight like two glass beads. There was no sign of Charlie or Josh.

Harry announced that he was tired and felt a bit sick and went back up to the campsite. Then Dig and Danny started having a burping contest. My head was aching from the beer and my legs were covered in goosebumps. It was time for bed.

I don't know what time Josh came back. I didn't hear him.

In the morning he was in a weird mood. When I asked him what time he came to bed he didn't answer. When Dad started singing "I will always love you", Josh stormed out of the tent. I noticed he had a love bite on his neck like a big strawberry.

Charlie's family were leaving at lunchtime. I dropped by their tent when they were packing up to say bye. Charlie hugged me. Just before she left she came and gave Josh a piece of paper with her address on and then they had a long intense snog in the adventure playground. Lots of younger kids were giggling at them but Josh didn't seem to care.

We all waved as Charlie's mum's car rumbled across the cattle-grid and out of the campsite.

13

Rachel

I got my photos developed after the holidays. There were some nice shots of Harry – Harry in his wet suit, Harry in his wellies, Harry with a mouthful of chocolate biscuits! There were some crazy ones of everyone on the cargo net in the adventure playground. There was one of Josh diving off the Roots that was just a pink blur. And there was a lovely one of Josh and Charlie in Harry's dinghy. I gave Josh that one and he pinned it on his bedroom notice board.

We were all surprised she didn't write. I'd expected daily letters and long smoochy phone calls. But there was nothing. Josh didn't mention her much though he was still wearing the friendship bracelet she'd made him. It was September. We were back at school. The hot weather was over. Everything was normal again.

Then, in the first week of October, a letter came. Dad went right over the top when he saw the Doncaster postmark and started singing "Whoa whoa whoa whoa-oh Mr Postman . . . Mr Postman look and see, if there's a letter, a letter for me . . ."

It was a Saturday morning. Josh got up late. Mum put the letter on the kitchen table beside his cereal bowl. It was gone eleven when he came down. I was making toast – watching him out of the corner of my eye. Josh opened the purple envelope and read the letter in silence.

"How is she?" I asked brightly. Josh didn't answer. He wolfed his breakfast down and barged out of the kitchen.

"Uh-oh," said Dad, coming in from the garden.

I go running on Saturday mornings. I'm in the local Harriers club. I went to the park down at the bottom of our road and was doing laps on the track there. There's a roller-blading park right next to the track with metal ramps and half pipes. Josh appeared on his roller blades. I waved to him but he didn't wave back. He was skating like a maniac, leaping off ramps and doing 360° turns in the air. I could hear the wheels of his skates clattering noisily on the tarmac. I lost count of the number of times he fell over. Every so often I could hear him swearing under his breath as I jogged past.

When I'd finished my laps I went and leaned on the railings by the skatepark. Josh was still hurtling about looking like an angry beetle in his shiny black skate helmet.

"Did she dump you?" I said, swigging on my water bottle. Josh didn't answer. "Is she seeing someone else?" Josh turned his back and skated away from me. I zipped up my tracksuit top.

"Whatever she said, it can't be *that* bad . . ." I called after him.

Josh spun round on his skates and glowered at me.

"Just *drop it* Rachel!" he shouted.

I know I shouldn't have read it – it was private, it was between Josh and Charlie only, it was none of my business.

Josh went out on his bike after lunch. He was gone ages. I kept going into his room to look for the letter and then telling myself I shouldn't and going back out again. I couldn't stop thinking about Josh's face when he'd told me to drop it. Josh is hardly ever that mad with me. Whatever Charlie had said was obviously one big deal. I looked at Charlie's smiling face on Josh's pinboard and felt a sudden rush of anger towards her. Anger that she could have such an effect on Josh. Anger that she could turn my twin brother against me. Silly cow! And why had it taken her till now to write to him?

There was no stopping me after that. Private or not I wanted to know what was going on. Me and Josh have never had secrets. The letter wasn't hard to find. It was stuffed into Josh's sock drawer. I opened the envelope and slowly slid the paper out. Charlie's handwriting was big and round. I started to read.

Dear Josh,

Hi! Sorry it's taken me so long to write to you. A lot has been going on since we got back from Kettlebeck and I haven't been feeling too well. There's no easy way to say this Josh so I'll just come out with it. I'm pregnant. At first I thought I had food poisoning or something because I kept being sick. Then I missed my period so I bought a kit at the chemist and did a test. I did the test twice and it was positive both times. Please write to me Josh. I'm really scared. I haven't told anyone yet and I don't know what to do. I would have phoned you but I didn't want to tell you over the phone in case someone heard.

Please write soon, Josh, and tell me you're not mad at me.

Write soon.

Lots of love, Charlie xxx

PS. I got my photos back from holiday and there's a great one of you on Dig's bike. I keep it under my pillow.

I read the letter through three times. Then I heard the garage door crash open downstairs. Josh threw his bike in with a clatter and opened the back door into the kitchen.

I stuffed the letter back into its envelope and

quickly closed the drawer. In the kitchen Mum was shouting at Josh.

"What a mess!" I heard her say. "Your new jeans are wrecked!"

I crept downstairs and peeped in the kitchen door. There was a huge rip in the knee of Josh's trousers and blood was trickling down his leg. Mum was rifling through the First Aid box.

"Why do you have to be so flipping reckless, Joshua?" Mum said. She slammed a box of elastoplasts down on the table. "I wish you'd ... I wish you'd *grow up!*"

Josh looked at me. He looked like a frightened little boy. Just for a moment I thought he was going to cry.

"I'll find a plaster, Mum," I said, stepping into the kitchen.

14

Rachel

Josh didn't mention Charlie's letter. For three days he hardly spoke to me at all. I kept hoping he'd come and confide in me – get it off his chest, let me in on the awful secret. But instead he was silent and moody. By Wednesday it was killing me so I started a conversation on the bus on the way to school.

"Have you written back to Charlie?" I said, trying to sound casual. We were at the front of the top deck. No one else was there.

"No," said Josh, wiping his finger across the misted-up windows.

"Do you think you will?" I said.

"Maybe," Josh said. It was obvious he didn't want to talk.

"Is something wrong?" I said.

"Why?" Josh said jumpily.

"You just seem a bit . . ." I couldn't think of the right word. Gloomy? Grumpy? Preoccupied?

"A bit what?" he said. His tone was defensive.

"You just don't seem yourself," I said.

"Rachel," said Josh impatiently, "I'm *fine*! Just get off my case!"

He started drawing a face on the window. Downstairs on the bus a baby started yelling. The sound of its cries tore right through me. I wondered if it had the same effect on Josh.

Josh didn't speak again for the rest of the journey. When we arrived at the school gates he met his friend Jamie and they went off talking about bikes. He didn't even say goodbye.

On Friday night I tried raising the subject again. Josh was in his room listening to music. I knocked on the door but he didn't hear me so I walked in anyway.

"Don't come in without knocking!" he said, spinning round in his chair.

"I *did* knock!" I said. "But you had your music on too loud!" Josh turned his back to me and drummed on his desk in time to the music. I reached over to his CD-player and turned the volume down. Josh glared at me.

"Have you got Charlie's address?" I said.

"Why?" said Josh.

"I want to write to her," I said, as innocently as I could.

"Why?" said Josh.

"I want to send her some of the photos," I said. Then I added, "Anyway, she's my friend too. I just want to write and say Hi – see how she is."

"She's fine!" Josh said angrily.

"Good," I said. "I'm glad. So have you got her address?"

"I lost it," Josh said, turning the music up loud again.

"What do you mean, you lost it?" I said.

"I lost the bit of paper," he said, "with her address on."

We were shouting at each other over the music. I turned the volume down again.

"*Rachel!*" said Josh, sounding annoyed.

"What about the letter?" I said. "Wasn't her address on that?" I knew it was. I saw it at the top of the page.

"I don't know where it is," Josh said feebly.

"Well look for it!" I said.

"*Rachel* – can't it wait?" Josh said. "I'm actually trying to listen to music. I'll find it *later*." He turned the music up again and closed his eyes. I wanted to hit him.

"I'll look for it then," I said. My voice was drowned out by the music. I started opening drawers – in his clothes cupboard, in his desk. I couldn't find it. It wasn't in the sock drawer where I'd seen it before. Suddenly Joshua opened his eyes and saw me searching. He jumped up from his chair and pressed Stop on the CD-player.

"What the hell do you think you're doing, Rachel?" he said.

"Looking for Charlie's letter," I said. "Seeing as how *you* won't look for it."

"Well do you think you could sod off?" he said angrily.

"Why is it such a big deal, Josh?" I said, eyeballing him.

"It's not a big deal Rachel. I just hate you rummaging about in my room. So *get out!*"

Just then I caught sight of something purple in Josh's waste-paper bin.

"What's that?" I said.

"What's what?" said Joshua.

"That! In the bin. Is that Charlie's letter?" I couldn't believe he'd put the letter in the bin. How could he?

Joshua glanced guiltily at the waste-paper basket.

"I don't . . ." He didn't finish what he was saying. I lunged forward and pulled the scrumpled paper from the bin.

"Yes, this is it," I said. "Dear Josh . . ."

Josh grabbed it out of my hand.

"Give me that!" he said.

"Calm down," I said. "Keep your hair on! Can you just tear the address off the top please?"

Josh turned his back so I couldn't see the letter and tore off the top couple of inches. He thrust the scrap of paper into my hand and scrunched the rest into a tight ball.

"Thanks," I said. Josh threw the ball of paper at

the bin. He did it in such an offhand way that I flipped.

"Is that supposed to make it go away?" I said.

"Make what go away?" said Josh.

"The baby!" I yelled.

"What baby?" Josh looked shocked.

"Charlie's baby," I said. "I *know* Josh. You can't hide it. You can't pretend it isn't happening . . ." I was really shouting at him. He looked astonished. Then he started yelling too.

"You read my letter!" he said. "How dare you go through my things! You nosy bitch!" I thought he was going to hit me.

Just at that moment Mum burst into the room.

"What *on earth* is going on?" she shouted. Josh froze. He looked at me with an air of desperation as if any moment I might blow his cover. I stared him out, but no matter how annoyed I felt with him there was *no way* I'd say anything to Mum. I folded my fingers shut over the scrap of purple paper and slipped it into my pocket.

"Nothing," I said. "I was just going," and I turned and walked quietly out of Joshua's bedroom. Mum looked surprised. I think she'd expected to referee in a fight.

"Well keep the noise down," she said. "It sounded like World War Three up here."

15

Rachel

Josh didn't mention the letter again and I said nothing more about it for the rest of the weekend. He acted like everything was normal, as if he'd blanked it out completely. He watched TV. He did his homework. He rode his bike. He helped Mum cook spaghetti bolognaise. He even vacuumed his room. He was exactly like he always is. No change.

On Monday I wrote to Charlie.

Dear Charlie,
Hi! I hope you won't mind me writing to you.

I have a confession to make. I read your letter to Josh – he didn't show it to me, I was nosy – sorry! So I know about you being pregnant.

I won't tell anyone so your secret is safe.

I think Josh is having difficulty getting his head round the news. I'm sure he'll write back to you soon.

I hope you're feeling OK. You must have had such a shock when you found out. What's it like being pregnant? Do you feel any different? Have you told your mum yet? Are you going to keep the baby?

Write back soon or ring me. My mobile number is 07794 316947.

Lots of love,

Rachel xx

PS. Hope you like the photos of Kettlebeck!

I sent her two photos of everyone on the cargo net and a picture of Josh sunbathing by the river. I didn't tell Josh I'd written.

A week later I had a letter from Charlie. It was in a purple envelope just like the one she sent Josh. I picked it up off the doormat before anyone else could see and read it sitting on the loo.

Dear Rachel,

I suppose I should be mad at you for reading my letter – but actually I'm quite relieved that you know.

Thanks for writing back.

Thanks as well for the photees. Josh looks as gorgeous as ever. Is he mad with me? Do you think he'll write soon?

You asked what it feels like to be pregnant. It's weird. At the moment I just feel sick all the time. I'm sick if I eat stuff – apart from wine gums which I want to eat all the time (so what's new?) – but I'm sick if I *don't* eat. I'm sick first thing in the morning when I get up and then I feel starving. Sometimes at school I feel as if I'm going to throw up so I have to go to the loo in a hurry, but I don't think anyone has sussed yet. I'm not fat or anything, and I don't look any different so it's a bit difficult to believe there's actually a baby inside me. I keep hoping there isn't and it's all a bad dream. Maybe if I did the test again it would be negative. Maybe I imagined it. Maybe if I concentrate really hard on how much I *don't* want a baby it will go away – just vanish, not grow or anything.

I haven't told my mum yet. I'm too scared. I almost told her yesterday when she gave me a hug and said I looked tired. But I couldn't make the words come out. I don't know how she'll react. What would your mum say?

I've thought about having an abortion. That's scary too. We watched a film in RE – they sucked the baby out with a vacuum thing. It was gross! There's a poster in the girls' changing rooms at school with a helpline number for pregnancy advice. I wrote the number down in my planner when no one was looking. I might ring it. What would you do?

Write back soon Rachel.
Lots of love,
Charlie xx

16

Rachel

Mum and Dad both work late on Wednesdays so Josh and I fix our own tea.

That was my chance to talk to Josh – when the house was empty and he couldn't hide himself away in his room. I cooked us noodles – Josh's favourite. We chatted about school and friends and homework – and noodles. I could feel Josh thawing until he was *almost* friendly again. As I served him a second helping of noodles I said, "Sorry I read your letter, Josh." He didn't answer. "It was wrong," I said. "I shouldn't have." Josh wound noodles round his fork.

"I'd *never* read your post," he said. I scraped the last noodles on to my plate.

"Yeah, well, like I said, I'm sorry," I said. Josh almost smiled.

"Can we talk about the baby?" I said tentatively.

"Oh, leave it, Rach," Joshua said, wiping soy sauce off his chin.

"Josh, you *can't* leave it!" I said.

"Rachel, don't start!" Josh said. But I'd started and I couldn't stop.

"Charlie's got a baby growing inside her and it's *yours*!" I said passionately.

"How do you *know* it's *mine*?" Josh said, slamming his fork down on the plate. "It could be anybody's. How do I know she hasn't slept with loads of people. She might be a right slag for all I know . . ."

"Charlie wouldn't . . ." I started to defend her but Josh interrupted me.

"How do *you* know Rachel?" Josh shouted. "You hardly know her. *I* hardly know her!"

"So how come you had sex with her?" I shouted. "I can't believe you were so stupid, Joshua. Haven't you heard of condoms?" I hadn't meant to say all that. It just came out.

"Oh get lost Rachel," Josh shouted. "As if *you* know what you're talking about!"

"I know that having unprotected sex makes babies!" I yelled.

"You don't say!" said Josh sarcastically.

"So how come you didn't think of that at Kettlebeck?" I said.

"It wasn't *my* fault!" Josh shouted. "It wasn't my idea to get drunk. Charlie was the one that went and got the beers. She was *asking* for it!"

"What?" I said savagely. "Asking to have a baby at fifteen? I don't *think* so, Josh!"

"She doesn't have to have it!" Josh said. "She can have an abortion!"

"What? Throw it in the bin?" I shouted. "Like you threw her letter in the bin? How convenient!"

Josh got up from the table and flung his plate into the sink.

"I don't need this," he said, heading for the door.

"Oh fine!" I said. "Just storm out – like you always do when things aren't going your way. Just run away, why don't you?"

"Shut up Rachel!" he said, walking out of the kitchen.

"I had a letter from Charlie too you know," I said. "She's dead scared. But she isn't planning on getting rid of the baby. She's got more guts than you have, Joshua Graham!"

Why was I so sure Charlie wouldn't get rid of it? She might have had an abortion already for all I knew.

I was following Josh up the stairs, ranting like a mad woman. He went into his bedroom and slammed the door but I opened it and barged in.

"Just piss off!" Josh shouted.

"Charlie wants to know if you're going to write to her," I said, wedging my foot in the door. "Or are you too chicken?"

"Why are you so concerned about this?" Josh said. He sounded infuriated. "It's none of your bloody business!"

"Josh," I said. "I'm your sister. This baby is my

flesh and blood. I'll be its *auntie* for God's sake! How can you say it isn't my business! And Mum and Dad – they'll be its *grandparents*!" I was almost in tears. I flopped down on to Joshua's bed, in exasperation.

Josh had his back to me, staring at the wall. I expected him to tell me to get out again, but he didn't. He said nothing. And then he said quietly,

"Are you going to tell them?"

"Who?" I said, "Mum and Dad?" He grunted a yes.

For a moment I felt like a poker player standing there with the ace of spades in my hand. I had all the power. If I told Mum and Dad, there was nothing Josh could do about it. They'd sort it. They'd make him face reality. There'd be no more pretending it wasn't happening.

But twins don't tell. That's the rule. Always has been. Always will. Twins stand together – whatever.

I looked at Josh's back. He was fiddling with his watch strap. I noticed he was still wearing the purple and green band around his wrist. His arms were still tanned but the colour was gradually fading like polished wood that's been in the sun too much.

"No," I said grudgingly. "No, I won't tell them."

Josh didn't turn round. He went on staring at the wall.

"Thanks," he said. His voice cracked a little as he spoke. "Thanks, Rach."

17

Joshua

Rachel annoys me so much! She thinks she's so damned sorted! She always thinks she knows what I'm thinking and how I'm feeling. And she's so flaming smug! Rachel Graham – Miss Perfect. Miss Self-Righteous. Miss I Would *Never* Do That!

"Why didn't you think of that at Kettlebeck?"

"Haven't you heard of condoms?"

"I can't believe you were that stupid?"

Yeah, well I wouldn't tell Rachel but *I* can't believe I was that stupid either. We just got carried away, in the heat of the moment. Washed along on a tide of coconut suntan oil and Stella Artois! It wasn't even especially nice. We were in a field, just downriver from the campsite. The grass was damp and lumpy and smelled of cow shit. I tore Charlie's top pulling it off so fast.

It was all over with so quickly. I don't know if Charlie enjoyed it – she didn't say. You always hope your first time will be really nice and special. Afterwards I just felt a bit stupid – and cold too.

I never thought she would get pregnant. That was the last thing on my mind. She was gorgeous and it was summer and I couldn't keep my hands off her. What did that have to do with babies? Sod all.

18

Rachel

Our birthday is in November – November 20th. Last year it was a Tuesday and it was snowing. Dad was singing more than usual. He's the only person I know who sings at the breakfast table.

"You're six-teen, you're beautiful, and you're mi-ine!" he sang, planting a kiss on the top of my head.

"Ringo Starr," he said, sitting himself down.

"Yes, Dad," I said, rolling my eyes.

Josh walked into the dining room looking gorgeous.

"Happy birthday darling," Mum said, kissing his cheek. He grinned broadly.

Then, noticing the snow outside the window, he said excitedly, "Snow! Maybe school will be cancelled!"

"I wish!" I said.

"Rach, will you build a snowman with me?" Josh said in a silly voice.

"You big kid!" said Mum, pouring a cup of coffee. Then, looking out at the garden, she said, "It doesn't look as if it's settling."

"Bad luck," I said.

"Sixteen," said Dad, going all sentimental. "I can hardly believe it. Doesn't time fly? It doesn't seem five minutes since they were in nappies, does it Sheila?"

"No, love," said Mum.

"Yes, Dad," said Josh, smiling at me.

"Now they're almost grown up," Dad continued. "You're legal now, Josh!" He gave Josh a cheeky wink. Josh caught my eye and looked away.

"Open your presents then," said Mum. She stirred milk into her coffee with a clink of the spoon.

Josh got a navy blue jumper from our auntie and I got some silver earrings. Mum and Dad gave us money. Josh was planning to buy a new bike with his, a Mongoose Fuzz Pro – apparently! I was saving up to go on holiday with my mate Nicola.

"Thanks, Mum," I said, giving her a hug. "Thanks, Dad."

"You're welcome," said Dad.

Just then I heard the thunk sound of the letterbox.

"Birthday post!" said Josh, jumping up from the table.

There was a big pile of cards and two parcels. The parcels were from Granny – orange shower gel for me and peppermint shower gel for Josh and a tenner wrapped around each bottle with a post-it note that said Buy yourself something nice!

"Bless!" said Josh. "Good old Granny!"

There was a card each from Grandma and Grandad (cheques enclosed), a card each from Dad's brother Pete (WH Smith vouchers enclosed) and a card each from Mum's friend Liz (book tokens enclosed). There were also two green envelopes – one for me and one for Josh. I recognized the handwriting instantly.

"Doncaster," said Dad, squinting at the postmark. "Oh that'll be . . . now what was she called? Nice girl, blonde hair, good at rounders, boy's name . . . Brian was it? Or Roger?"

"Charlie," I said, giving Dad a look. I opened the envelope addressed to me. The card had a bog-eyed rabbit with a flower in its teeth.

Happy Birthday Rachel, lots a luv Charlie xxx

Josh didn't open his. He slid it under his new jumper and helped himself to a piece of toast.

"Will you want more after that?" Mum said.

"Yes please," Josh said. "Can I have another slice?" He spooned a big dollop of marmalade on to his plate.

Mum went into the kitchen to make more toast. Then the phone rang and Dad went out into the hall. Josh took the chance to hiss at me, "How did she know it was my birthday?"

"Well I told her it was *mine* on November 20th so she wouldn't need a Maths degree to work out it was yours too!" I said sarcastically.

"Don't be a smart arse, Rachel!" said Josh angrily.

"So!" He brandished the green envelope at me like a weapon. "Is this supposed to make me feel guilty or something?"

"Feel how you like!" I said, sipping coffee. "It's only a birthday card, Joshua, not a marriage proposal. Don't overreact!"

Hearing our raised voices, Mum came back in.

"Don't squabble on your birthday, you two!" she said in a weary voice. She put a slice of hot toast on Josh's plate. Josh scowled at me.

I looked out of the window at the snow falling like handfuls of torn paper.

19

Joshua

We went out the Saturday after our birthday – six of us, me and Rachel and Mum and Dad and my best mate Jamie and Rachel's best friend Nicola. We went bowling and then for a pizza.

I was a bit off form. Jamie got four strikes and won by miles. Nicola's ball kept going into the gully and missing the skittles altogether. She seemed to get worse the longer we played. Jamie was trying to help her improve her technique! He kept giving her advice and commenting on her throwing action. I reckon he fancies her. She is nice looking. But nothing like as nice looking as Charlie.

I hadn't told Jamie about Charlie. At least, not the whole story. He saw the photos of course.

"Bloody hell!" he said, gawping at a picture of her sunbathing. We'd been sitting on my bed the week we came back from Kettlebeck looking at Rachel's pictures. Jamie had got too much sun in Majorca and his sunburn was peeling all over my duvet.

"Gross! Your legs have got dandruff," I said, brushing away flakes of skin.

"Did you kiss her?" Jamie asked. I nodded. "You

lucky bugger!" he said. I didn't tell him the rest. Even by then it all felt a bit unreal. And now I had no intention of telling him she was pregnant. He'd take the piss something awful.

At the restaurant it was "Eat all you can!" so I ate all the pizza I could. I thought Jamie would be sick, he ate so much. Dad proposed a toast with a glass of Heineken. "To Joshua and Rachel," he said. "Happy birthday! Sweet sixteen and never been kissed!"

"That's not what I heard," said Jamie with a smirk.

Across the table Rachel was giving me one of her looks.

20

Rachel

A few days after my birthday Charlie rang me on my mobile. It wasn't great timing. I was in River Island after school, looking at the jewellery with Nicola.

Charlie was crying.

"What's wrong?" I said.

"I don't know what to do," Charlie said. I could hardly hear her through the sobbing and the signal wasn't very good.

"Do you like this?" Nicola said, holding a silver pendant up in front of me.

"Hang on," I mouthed to her.

"Who is it?" Nicola whispered. I waved my hand at her to go away and she pulled a huffy face.

"Charming," she said, walking back to the necklace stand.

"I can't really hear you," I said to Charlie. "I'm in a shop. I'm just going to take you outside."

I went outside and sat on a bench in the precinct. It was really cold and almost dark.

"Charlie?" I said. "Sorry about that. Are you still there?"

"Yes," said Charlie with a loud sniff.

"Has something happened?" I said. "I mean something new?"

"I rang the helpline," Charlie spluttered.

"The pregnancy one?" I said.

"Mmm-hmm," Charlie said vaguely.

"What did they say?" I said. What *do* they say? I had no idea.

"I've made an appointment to go and talk to them about an abortion next Tuesday, after school," Charlie said. "But I don't know if I've done the right thing. I mean it's killing something isn't it?"

"I suppose so," I said. "But if you think it's for the best then maybe . . ." Maybe what? Maybe that makes it OK? I didn't know what to say. Charlie's letter had asked what I'd do. What *would* I do? Would I want to have a baby at Charlie's age? At my age? Would I cope? Would I be any good at it? I'd jumped down Josh's throat when he said Charlie could get an abortion. Talked about throwing things in the bin. But lots of people had abortions. Surely it was better than having a baby you didn't want. Or a baby you couldn't begin to look after.

"Rachel?" said Charlie. "Are you still there?"

"Yeah," I said.

"What should I do?"

"Did they tell you anything about it – like how they do it?" I said.

"Not really," said Charlie. "But she did say I was

too far on for the pill thing and I'd have to have the surgical procedure."

"What's the pill thing?" I asked.

"There's a pill they can give you to make you have a miscarriage but you can only have it up to nine weeks."

"How many weeks are you?" I asked.

"About sixteen I think," Charlie said. Sixteen weeks already! That was four months. Babies only took nine months to be full sized. I asked another question.

"Does it cost a lot – the operation I mean?" I said.

"She didn't say," Charlie said. "She said they tell you everything you need to know at the consultation."

"I think you should go for the appointment then," I said. "Then you can find out more and decide what you want to do."

"What does Josh want me to do?" Charlie said. Did she want me to be brutally honest? Not over the phone. Not when she was crying. I lied.

"He wants you to do what's best for *you*," I said.

Nicola had come out of River Island and was walking towards me.

"I'd better go," I said. "Phone me again," I said.

"Thanks Rachel," Charlie said. "You're a mate." The phone went dead.

"Who *was* it?" Nicola said.

"No one," I said stupidly.

"Oh sure . . . the invisible man," said Nicola sarcastically.

"I can't tell you," I said, slipping my phone into my bag. "It's . . . well it's confidential."

"Fine," said Nicola with a shake of her head. "*Be* secretive then!"

We crossed the road to catch the bus.

A week later there was a letter from Charlie.

Dear Rach,

I went to the clinic today for my appointment. It wasn't a bit like I expected. I thought it would be all white and clinical and creepy. But it was nice and friendly with a big comfy sofa and flowers on the desk. I talked to a woman called Carol. She was really nice. She gave me lots of information and showed me leaflets. I had to fill in a big questionnaire. This is the deal: I could have what they call a surgical abortion where they remove the contents of the womb by suction. Because my pregnancy is quite advanced I'd need a general anaesthetic but I could be in and out in a day and it wouldn't hurt. Afterwards it would be like having a heavy period for a few days, but that would be that. No baby. I can see a counsellor if I want to but I don't have to. It's quite expensive. It would cost about £500 if I went to a private clinic – more if I had to stay in overnight. I know Mum would pay if I told her, but I haven't told her yet. I might get an abortion free on the NHS, but I'd have to tell our family doctor – and some hospitals won't do them, anyway.

When I said I wasn't sure if it was right Carol asked if I had religious beliefs that made the decision difficult for me. I'd never really thought of myself as someone with religious beliefs! But the more I think about it, the more I think taking a baby's life away just because I don't want to mess my life up seems wrong – selfish, anyway. I don't know if that's religious or not. What d'you reckon? Carol didn't mention babies once. She just talked about "the contents of my womb" and treatment and procedures.

I think I've made my mind up. I'm going to keep the baby. I told Carol I needed more time to think and she said to get in touch if I wanted to proceed further. But I know I won't. Do you think I've done the right thing? Will Josh be pleased? I'm still scared. But this way seems better. Write soon, Rach. It was good to talk to you the other night. Thanks.

Lots of love Charlie xx

21

Rachel

Charlie wrote again in the middle of December. She'd had a scan. She sent the scan photo. It looked like those satellite photos they show on the weather.

I saw its heart beating.

she wrote,

And you could see its fingers.

I looked hard at the picture. I couldn't see anything that looked like fingers – only patches of snow and dark shadows like the surface of the moon.

It was wriggling about all over the place,

she said.

And guess what? It's a boy!

I wondered how they could tell when everything looked so fuzzy.

I'm eighteen weeks already. Nearly half way. I can't believe how quickly time is going. Tell Josh to hurry up and write.

I took off my school uniform, slipped the letter safely into a drawer and went downstairs.

It's a boy! It's a boy!

The words were going round and round in my

head like the riff of a song. Mum was home early from work. She was icing a chocolate cake at the kitchen bench.

"December 13th," she said, looking up. "Sam's birthday."

I felt bad for not remembering. Mum always makes a cake on his birthday.

"He'd have been ten," she said. I gave her a hug. Silently she took some candles out of a tin and counted out ten.

"Can I help with tea?" I said.

"No, it's all done," Mum said.

"I love you Mum," I said, giving her another hug.

"Don't, you'll make me cry," she said, wiping her eyes.

I was nine when Sam died. It was only a few days after his birthday. There were still balloons in the house. Sam was in the back of the car strapped into a kids' seat. Mum was driving him home from playgroup. They were at the traffic lights on the dual carriageway. Someone ran a red light and smashed into the side of our car. Sam was dead when the ambulance arrived.

Mum has a pale scar across her cheek where a shard of glass got lodged.

I remember Dad's face when he met us at the

school gates. He was ghastly pale with a haunted look in his eyes.

"Where's Mum?" I asked. "Why aren't you at work?"

"Where's Sam?" Josh said. He was usually in his buggy with Mum.

Dad didn't tell us till we got home. He made us a drink of Ribena and some jam sandwiches and we all sat on the sofa in the lounge. Josh made a fuss because he wanted to watch Children's TV.

"Not today, Josh," Dad said quietly.

Our sandwiches sat uneaten on the plate.

We'd put the Christmas tree up early that year. I remember staring at a salt dough Santa spinning in the draught from the door. I stared at it as hard as I could so I wouldn't cry.

I cried later, sitting on my bed, hugging Pooh Bear. Josh didn't cry at all. He went outside without a coat and rode his bike fiercely up and down the path till it was pitch dark.

I wrote to Charlie after tea.

Dear Charlie,
Thanks for both your letters and the scan photo. I wasn't sure which way up it went but the baby is beautiful – of course!

I'm glad you decided to have it. I think you're really brave. Are you glad it's a boy?

Can I tell Josh?

You sound much happier. Have you told your mum? And what did she say? Are you absolutely *definitely* going to keep the baby? Are you fat yet?

Thanks for the birthday card – Josh says thanks for his too. He's planning to write to you soon but you know what boys are like!

Have you got e-mail? My e-mail address is rachelbabe@lineone.net. No one else reads it so don't worry about privacy.

I'm saving up to go to Tenerife with my mate Nicola after exams next summer.

Write soon, lots of love Rachel xxxx

22

Joshua

Mum made a cake again – for Sam – with candles and everything. I wish she wouldn't do that. It's so morbid! He's been dead for years. He's been dead so long that I can hardly remember him. I never think about him. Never.

Mum just upsets herself making a cake every year on his birthday. It's like she's punishing herself for him not being here any more – like she can't forgive herself for the crash.

The past is the past. People should forget.

23

Rachel

I checked my e-mail after school when no one was around. Josh was at Jamie's house and Mum and Dad were still at work. There was a message from Charlie.

Dear Rach,

I'm writing this in the library at school. Our modem broke and Mum can't afford to replace it so I can't e-mail you from home.

Thanks for your letter.

Yes, I'm glad it's a boy. Knowing what sex it is makes it seem more real.

Yes, I'm definitely *going to keep it.*

Yes, I told my mum.

I had to. I was so scared and I was starting to get fat. Mum went mad and yelled at me for being stupid and irresponsible. She said I was ruining my life and I should have an abortion. Then she apologized and cried all over me. Then she phoned the doctor and booked me in for checks and blood tests and things. She hasn't told Steve yet. She isn't sure how he'll take it.

And Dominic doesn't know. The other day he said I looked fat.

I told him he was ugly. At least I could lose weight – but he'd always be ugly! He swore at me so Mum sent him to his room. It was nice that she took my side for once! She's being really nice to me – making me big salads and telling me to drink lots of milk. But she keeps asking me if I want to think again about abortion before it's too late. I think that's what she wants me to do, but she doesn't say it in as many words. It would be neater. More convenient. Am I being stupid? Is it madness to keep it? I don't know – but I've made my mind up.

Tenerife will be nice – you lucky woman. The baby is due on May 29th so I don't think I'll be joining you!

Ooops! Mrs Shaw the librarian is coming.

See ya, C

I looked on my calendar – on the forward planner. May 29th – that was the week before exams started. Wednesday. I counted backwards to August. Forty weeks. Charlie was four and a half months pregnant. What did babies look like at four and a half months? Did they look human? What did Charlie's baby look like? Did it look like Josh?

24

Rachel

In the Christmas holidays Josh went out on a date with Kirsty Warner. I was *so* mad with him. But I was even madder that he didn't *tell* me! Nicola told me. She saw them in a pub in town. Kirsty Warner is in Year Ten. She's got bushy eyebrows and a big bum.

I stormed into his room. It was a Saturday and I'd just been Christmas shopping. I'd bought Charlie a necklace with a sparkly letter C on it. I plonked my carrier bags down on Josh's carpet on top of sweaty clothes and crumpled magazines.

"How could you?" I said.

"How could I what?" Josh said, all innocent. He was reading a bike magazine.

"You know!" I said, glowering at him.

"I don't *know* Rach," he said calmly.

"Go out with Kirsty Warner! She's a right cow!" I yelled. Josh smiled patronisingly. He was wearing his birthday jumper. It looked really good on him.

"She's not a cow actually, Rach," he said reasonably. "She's very nice. And I don't see what it's got to do with you!"

"It's got everything to do with me. You've got no

right to date someone else!" I said.

"How d'you work that one out Rachel?" Josh said. He was deliberately acting dumb to wind me up.

"What about Charlie?" I squawked.

"What about her?" Josh said. I wanted to slap him.

"She's pregnant!" I said.

"So?" said Josh provocatively.

"So, she's *pregnant*!" I said again, only louder.

"What are you saying Rach?" Josh said. "That Charlie Lewis is pregnant so I'm not allowed to see anyone else ever again even though Charlie's in Doncaster which is flipping miles away? It's hardly a practical arrangement is it Rachel?"

"You could at least phone her or write or *some*thing!" I shouted. It was the first time I'd been in Josh's room for a while. I noticed that the photo of him and Charlie had disappeared from his notice board. I wondered if he'd put *that* in the bin too.

"Rachel will you back off!" Josh said. "You're acting like you're my mum or something – *lighten up*!"

"You're in denial big style!" I said, flinging a cushion at him.

"Don't give me that pyscho-babble bullshit!" Josh said scornfully.

I snatched up my carrier bags from the bedroom floor.

"I don't suppose you'll buy her anything for

Christmas either!" I said and I marched out of the room.

"Why should I?" Josh shouted after me.

"Because you *slept* with her!" I yelled.

"I wouldn't call it *sleeping* Rachel!" he shouted, banging his door behind me.

Mum and Dad were out which was just as well. We were shouting so loud the whole street probably heard. I went into my room and slammed the door. I'd bought a CD for Josh for Christmas. I took it out of the carrier bag. It was still wrapped in cellophane. For a moment I was tempted to throw it out of the window and watch it shatter on the drive below. But I didn't. Why didn't I? Maybe because I love Josh. Even when I hate him I love him! Even when he's acting like a complete jerk! That's the trouble. If I didn't love him I wouldn't have been so angry.

I put the CD in my secrets drawer – with Charlie's necklace and all her letters. Mum and I have an agreement that she never goes in there. I hope she never breaks it. Then there'll really be trouble.

25

Rachel

After Christmas I went to the library in town to get some books about pregnancy. I wanted to know what the baby looked like – which bits of it had already formed? How big was it? I can't imagine what it must be like to have a human being growing inside you. I'd never thought about it before. It's pretty mind-blowing!

I found a brilliant book with photos of babies in the womb, and another called *Pregnancy, Your Questions Answered*. When I got home I looked on the calendar. Charlie was twenty weeks by then – five months pregnant. The photo book had pictures of babies at five months and they were *perfectly* formed. They had fingernails and eyebrows and hair and everything. The book said they were 25 centimetres long, half the length of an average newborn baby. I looked on my ruler – 25 centimetres was the distance from my elbow to my wrist.

Mum walked in when I was looking at the book. I jumped a mile.

"What's that?" Mum said. It would have looked fishy to hide it.

"Research!" I said quickly, trying not to look too shifty. "For school, for PSE," I lied.

Mum leaned over my shoulder. My heart was racing. I wondered if she could hear it.

"Fantastic photos," she said, leafing through the book. She stroked the back of my hair absent-mindedly as she looked. I unclenched a little.

"Dinner's almost ready," she said.

"Thanks," I answered. Then before I could stop myself I said, "What's it like being pregnant?"

Mum sat down on the bed. She likes being asked questions like that. She's good at talking about stuff – stuff like periods and feelings – deep personal stuff.

"It's amazing," she said.

"Is it nice?" I asked.

"Mostly," said Mum. Then she said, "So much changes. Your body changes – your shape, the things you like eating, your sleeping patterns – even your hair feels different. And your emotions are all over the place like a yo-yo – terrified one minute, then elated, and weepy and . . . impatient! SO impatient!"

"Can you feel the baby?" I said. Charlie hadn't said anything about that.

"Not at the beginning," Mum said. "Round about twenty weeks or so you start feeling little fluttering feelings – and then, by the end the baby thrashes about all over the place. You can actually see it – when you're in the bath and things – lumps and bumps appearing and disappearing as the baby rolls about. It's a bit like watching someone thrashing about under a duvet!"

"Wow!" I said. "Were you *really* fat when you were pregnant?"

"I wasn't so bad with Sam," Mum said. "But with *you two* I was like a *whale*! You were both big babies. I think you must have been pretty squashed in there!"

"No room for Josh to ride his bike!" I said, laughing.

Thinking about it I can remember when Mum was having Sam. We used to put our hands on her tummy to feel the baby kick. Josh used to say that meant it was a boy and it would be good at football.

"The worst bit is needing the loo all the time," Mum said. "And piles!"

"Oooh man!" I said, wincing. "Does everyone get piles?" I thought of Charlie.

"Only the unlucky ones," Mum said. "And the ones called Emma."

"What?" I said. She'd lost me there.

"Emma-roid!" said Mum with a belly laugh.

She stood up to go. Just as she reached the door I found myself saying, "Mum? What would you say if I told you I was pregnant?"

Mum froze in her tracks. She turned round and looked me in the eye and said in a deadly serious voice, "Rachel . . .?"

"I'm not – of course not!" I said, feeling myself blush. "I'm just curious."

Mum weighed up my face. I've never been any good at lying, Mum knows that. She must have decided she believed me because then she said, "I'd throw you out on to the street!"

"Seriously Mum," I said. "Would you make me have an abortion?"

"I wouldn't *make* you," she said. "I might recommend it as an option."

"Would you think it was for the best?" I said.

"Maybe, but not necessarily." Mum sat down on the bed again. "Sometimes, at work, I see girls as young as thirteen having babies. Some of them are a disaster area and an abortion would have been better for everyone. But some of them are great mothers."

Mum's a family social worker. She works a lot with kids in care.

"What about boys?" I said. "Are they ever great dads?"

"Sometimes," Mum said. "Not often, I have to say. Most often they cut and run and leave it all to the women. But not always."

My heart started pounding faster and faster. Should I tell Mum about Josh and Charlie? It was an ideal opportunity. Mum would understand. She'd handle it right. She'd help Josh to come to terms with everything. She'd help him to be a great dad. He'd listen to her. I know he would . . .

I opened my mouth to speak but a voice in my head said, "Twins don't tell! That's the rule . . ."

Suddenly Mum jumped up. I'd missed my chance. There was a nasty smell drifting up the stairs.

"Damn!" she said, "Something's burning!" And she shot out of the door and ran down the stairs.

26

Joshua

Rachel had some books in her room about babies. I'm sure she only put them there to make me feel bad. I looked at one of them while she was out. It had all these photographs of embryos. They looked more like fish than humans – strange half-formed pink tadpoley things. Looking at them made me feel sick.

Everywhere I go at the moment I see pregnant women and babies in prams. I'm sure there never used to be so many. Babies, babies, babies. It feels like the whole world is having babies. It's like a blooming zoo!

I took the photo of Charlie down off the wall. I put it in the drawer – face down. I couldn't handle her grinning at me all the time. It made me feel bad. We both look so cheerful and happy. I wonder what she looks like now. I don't want to think about it. I don't want to think about her at all.

I took the band off my wrist. It was starting to annoy me – when it got wet in the shower and things. Charlie said I had to wear it for ever. But for ever is a long time.

I nearly put it in the bin but nosy Rachel would probably have fished it out again. So I put it in the drawer too – with the photo. Relics of a forgotten summer. Forgotten. *Forgetting*, anyhow . . .

27

Rachel

In January we had mocks. I worked pretty hard for them but Josh just pratted about. He kept going off with Jamie to build bike ramps and staying out for hours. Even when Mum and Dad *thought* he was revising he was just reading *Ride* magazine and sketching ramps. Since he got his new BMX, bikes are all he thinks about. He's even got a *Ride* calendar with photos of stunt bikes for every month of the year. He's obsessed!

I hadn't mentioned Charlie since our argument before Christmas, although she wrote to me a lot – or e-mailed me during IT. She said she was getting more and more pissed off with not hearing from Josh and she'd started slagging him off in her letters. I was getting sick of sticking up for him and telling lies about how he felt so as not to hurt her feelings. She said she'd talked to her mum about him. Her mum said he was acting like a typical man – ducking responsibility and leaving women to pick up the pieces. Charlie's dad walked out on her mum just after she had Dominic so she's bitter about men. I wonder how Steve feels when she says stuff like that. Not all men are unreliable. Dad isn't.

So how come Josh is?

Charlie said she was getting fatter and none of her clothes fit.

I look disgusting she wrote. She said her boobs were as big as melons and had gone all hard and sore. She said people had found out at school and lots of kids were giving her a hard time and calling her "Slag" and "Slapper". Someone had written on the board "Charlie Lewis is up the duff!" She even said some of her teachers were being snotty with her and treating her like a bad smell. She said she was beginning to wonder if she should have just bitten the bullet and gone to the abortion clinic early on before any one else knew. But now it was too late.

It's all right for Josh she said. *He can keep it a secret as long as he likes. But it's hard to keep a secret when you look like Tinky Winky!*

Josh's mocks results were so bad he was grounded. He was mad as anything. Jamie was apparently making a series of dirt jumps called a six-pack down at Smithies Field. Josh was desperate to be there. Mum and Dad said he needed to sort his priorities out. Tell me about it!

At the end of January Charlie e-mailed me from school.

Dear Rachel,

Today I'm 24 weeks. The baby is kicking now. When I'm lying in bed at night I can feel it inside me. It's scary – but fantastic too.

Sorry I've moaned a lot recently.

And sorry I was horrible about Josh. I love him really! Luv Charlie

Why does she love Josh? He's acting like such an arse!

I looked in the book. It said:

Twenty-four weeks is the legal limit for abortion in Great Britain. After that date a pregnancy cannot legally be terminated, unless the mother's life is at risk.

I didn't reckon Charlie's life was at risk. So that was that. There was no way back. The baby would be born whether Josh liked it or not.

28

Joshua

After I messed up my exams I was grounded for three weeks. Then Mum took pity on me and let me go out on a date with Kirsty Warner. Rachel was furious! I've been out with Kirsty a few times – on and off. Nothing heavy. She's OK. She makes me laugh. I don't fancy her that much – not the way I fancied Charlie anyway. To be honest I'd rather have gone dirt ramping with Jamie but that apparently was out of the question since, according to Mum and Dad, too much biking is the cause of my academic downfall.

It was a bit of a strange date. We went to her auntie's house to babysit. Kirsty said there'd be no baby – just a video and a frozen pizza. She babysat for her cousin all the time. It was a doddle, she said. He never usually woke up.

No such luck. We'd only been there twenty minutes when the baby started to yell. We hadn't even finished watching the trailers and the pizza was still in its box. Kirsty went and got the baby and brought it downstairs. It was all red in the face and bursting its lungs.

"I'll go and get his bottle," she said. "Here, you hold him." She handed the baby to me. I'd never held a baby before in my life. It was all hot and stiff and its arms and legs were thrashing about. Then suddenly it puked all down my shirt – like a spurting yellow fountain.

"Help!" I shouted, holding it as far away from me as I could. "Kirsty! It's been sick!" I yelled.

She came in from the kitchen. When she saw me she laughed.

"I'm glad you think it's funny!" I said. At least the baby had at last stopped yelling. It had begun to do my head in.

"I'll change him," she said, taking him from me. "Looks like I need to change *you* too!"

"Ha ha, very funny," I said crossly. Kirsty went away and changed the baby's clothes. I took my shirt off. It stank. I felt a bit stupid with a bare chest so I put my coat on. Kirsty came back, carrying the baby in a new suit with purple hippos all over it.

"Groovy gear," I said, making an effort. She smiled. She sat down beside me on the sofa with the baby on her knee and started jigging it about and pulling daft faces.

"Don't make it sick again," I said.

"He likes it," she said, grinning stupidly.

"Are we going to watch the film or what?" I said impatiently.

"Soon," she said. Then she said in a silly voice, "How big is Nathan? SO BIG!" and she stretched her arms up high.

The baby started chuckling. It looked alarmingly wide awake. I wanted my pizza.

"You said it would be in bed," I said.

"It's not an *it* it's a *he*," Kirsty said stroppily. "And you can't programme them to go to sleep when you want them to, you know!"

"Sorry," I said.

"That's OK," said Kirsty with a half smile.

"Here . . . you hold him," she said. "I'll go and put the pizza in the oven." She held him out to me.

"What if he's sick again?" I asked feebly.

"You'll mess your coat up too," Kirsty said matter-of-factly. "Take him," she said.

I took him and sat him on my knee like she'd done. He'd relaxed now and gone all soft and floppy. His head kept wobbling about like those model dogs in the backs of cars. Reaching out his tiny starfish hand he took hold of my finger and gripped it tight. I noticed how little his fingernails were. Then all of a sudden he did this enormous grin. Something happened in my stomach – a sort of falling feeling like when you go too fast over a humpback bridge.

The baby was still grinning when Kirsty came back.

"Aaah!" she said. "He likes you. You're a natural, Josh. You'd make a dead nice dad."

That was it. When she said that, I knew I needed to leave. I had a churning feeling in my stomach and my hands went all sweaty.

"Here, *you* have him," I said, handing him abruptly back to her. "I'm actually not feeling too well. I'm going to have to go." Kirsty looked surprised.

"But what about the pizza?" she said.

"Sorry," I said. "I don't think I could manage it." I felt sick as it was. Maybe it was the smell of the baby vomit on my shirt.

I left Kirsty standing at the door with a bundle of baby in her arms. I didn't kiss her or anything.

"Thanks for the date," she said sarcastically as I walked away down the path.

29

Rachel

There was deep snow at the end of February. School was closed for the day and Dad couldn't get to work. It was Mum's day off anyway so we all went sledging down at Smithies Field.

Josh and I took turns to go down the hill while Mum and Dad built a crazy-looking snowman with big biceps and straggly grass for hair. Then Dad did some mad runs on the sledge lying on his chest. The snow sprayed up in front of him like a boat's bow wave and coated his eyelashes white.

"OK, double runs now," Dad said. "Girls first. Come on Sheila, you haven't been down yet."

Mum and I went down the slope together clutching the string on the front of the sledge. With the extra weight we went really fast. At the bottom I leaned sideways to miss a tree and we rolled off into a snowdrift.

"Whoooo!" said Mum, standing up and dusting herself off. There was no stopping her after that. She just wanted to sledge and sledge.

"Yo!" said Josh. "Mum discovers extreme sport!"

Mum was getting on the sledge with Josh – she

was at the front, cradled inside Josh's arms. Josh had a huge grin on his face. They set off down the hill. Mum was screaming like she was on a roller coaster.

"Look out, Mum!" Josh yelled as they hurtled towards a tree. He wrapped his arms round Mum's shoulders and leaned hard to the right. Mum had her eyes shut tight.

"Saved you," said Josh as they slid to a halt. Mum beamed.

After that Mum and Dad went down several times together squealing like big kids.

Josh and I stood on the slope and pelted them with snowballs as they shot past. Josh managed to hit Dad and knock his hat off.

"I'll get you Joshua Graham!" Dad shouted. "Just you wait!"

Dad was coming back up the hill, towing the sledge behind him. His grey hair was wild and wavy from the melted snow.

"You and me now Josh," Dad said. "Father and son ride!" He clasped Josh round the shoulders and then, snatching the hat off his Josh's head, he rubbed snow in his face. "I'll get you for that!" Josh said.

They went to the top of the hill and clambered on to the sledge. Dad was singing "Life is a roller coaster . . . gotta ride it!" as they gathered speed. They went down the slope so fast that they couldn't stop at the bottom. They were heading straight for the stone wall that borders the lane.

"Next stop, casualty," said Mum under her breath. Just in time, Dad yelled, "Aban-don ship!" and they threw themselves off the sledge as it clattered into the wall and broke in two.

Dad and Josh were in deep snow, face down and coated in white like iced buns. Josh jumped up and quickly started lobbing snowballs at Dad. So Dad grabbed a handful of snow and thrust it down the back of Josh's coat. A big snow fight followed. We ran down the hill to join in. There was lots of laughing and threats of revenge. Finally Dad grabbed Josh's legs and rugby tackled him to the ground.

"Ref-er-ee!" said Mum with joke indignation.

Dad and Josh stood up.

"Truce!" said Dad, holding out his hand to Josh. Josh smiled. Then Dad opened his arms wide and gave Josh a hug. Josh looked uncomfortable. He pulled away and shook himself.

As he turned I saw he was wiping his eyes. I couldn't tell if he was wiping away snow or tears.

"Are you OK?" I asked. Josh rubbed his nose hard. It was red from the cold.

"Fine," he said, looking away.

30

Rachel

The day after the sledging I had a long letter from Charlie.

Dear Rach,

How are you? Well done for doing so well in your mocks. How did Josh do?

Mine were all right. I did much better than everyone expected and managed an A* in English. I even got a C in French which will just show stupid Mr Fowler, who's been treating me like a leper.

Things are a bit better at school. People have stopped calling me names. But being pregnant really sorts out who your real friends are. Lots of people who I thought were my mates now just ignore me completely. My best mate Gemma is being so cool though. She keeps telling me to sit down and bringing me tubes of wine gums!

Mum is still being nice to me – nicer than she's been for years. She bought the baby a really cute babygrow at the weekend with little Bart Simpsons all over it. My grandma is being nice too – the line-dancing one, Grandma Jean. She was shocked at first and tutted a lot and rolled her eyes. "That's what you get for having a pierced navel!" she said. As if? But now she's being kind and supportive. She says us women have to stick together. "Times have changed," she says. "It's even happening in Coronation Street!" She says she'll punch Josh if he ever shows his face – but don't tell him. She's pretty scary, especially in her rhinestone boots.

Even Dominic is being nice to me – which is weird! – he hasn't hit me for ages. He says having a baby in the house will be "wicked!" and he'll be its Uncle Dom. What a scary thought!

Steve's a bit cagey with me. I don't think he's angry about it – I just think he's not sure what to say or how to act with me. Like I've crossed over from being a little girl into being a woman and he's a bit freaked. Perhaps he's worried that having a baby in the house will make Mum broody and she'll want one too!

I've decided I'm going to leave school after exams and go to the Tech to do A Levels. They have a crèche there that the baby can go in and they treat you like a grown-up – unlike school!

Mum says she'll look after the baby on Friday nights so I can go clubbing.

So things are looking pretty good, considering.

The only bad things are
1. Looking like a fat cow
2. Having puffed up ankles like balloons
3. Needing to pee all the time

And Josh . . . It's getting me down that I still haven't heard from him. Is he OK? Does he hate me? Is he still alive?

Does he ever mention me?

Should I phone him, or write another letter?

Tell me what to do Rach?

Lots a luv Charlie xxxxxxxx

Josh isn't wearing his friendship bracelet any more. He must have cut it to get it off. I bet it's in the bin – cold-hearted sod! So much for "for ever". I won't tell Charlie. That would be the last straw.

31

Joshua

It rained a lot in March. The ground was super soft –
ideal for digging. Jamie and I were making this run of
ramps, at the bottom of Smithies Field, in the woods
near Jamie's house. It was a six-pack – a four foot
double, flowing into a five foot step-up, and on into a
six foot table top. It was class! Since I got my new
bike I'd been riding it a lot at the skate park – while it
was winter and the ground was wet and icy. It's a
great ride. It's light but it can take the hits and it runs
quick on concrete even though the tyres are built for
dirt. I couldn't wait to jump the new trails when the
weather dried out a bit.

We were digging one Sunday afternoon when it
started tipping it down with rain.

"Let's go to my house and play on Driver," Jamie
said. We dumped our bikes in his garage and were
making toasties in the kitchen when his mum walked
in. I hadn't been to Jamie's for ages – what with being
grounded and stuff.

Jamie's mum looked different from usual. She was
much fatter than usual, and she was walking as if
she had a bad back or something.

"Hello Joshua," she said, bending down and taking some clothes out of the washing machine. "How are you?"

"Fine," I said, trying not to stare at her.

"Can we eat that chocolate cake in the fridge, Mum?" said Jamie. There's always good cake at Jamie's house.

"Yeah, OK," his mum said, "but leave some for me." She straightened up and patted her stomach. Then she picked up the laundry basket and went out of the room.

Jamie opened the fridge and took out the remains of a chocolate gateau.

"Want some?" he said. I nodded.

"Jamie," I said as the penny slowly dropped. "Your mum's not . . . you know . . . is she?" I couldn't say the word. Jamie said it for me.

"Pregnant?" he said. "Yeah – didn't I tell you?"

"Isn't she a bit old?" I said. Okay, It was a bit of a rude thing to say. But Jamie's mum's got grey hair and he's got a sister at university.

"Forty-four," Jamie said. He looked a bit embarrassed for a moment then he grinned. "I don't think they planned it," he said.

"God!" I said. "D'you mind?"

"Nah, I think it's great," Jamie said. "I can't wait. I love babies."

Why did he love babies? I pictured Kirsty's cousin

red and wailing and vomiting down my shirt. Then I thought of Charlie. I tried to picture her pregnant, like Jamie's mum, but I couldn't. When I thought of her she was standing on the Roots in a black crop top with water dripping off her hair.

"Here," said Jamie, handing me a plate of cake. "Do you want a fork?"

"Cheers," I said. Then I said, "Jamie?" Jamie was scraping chocolate cream off the blade of a knife. Was this the moment? Was I going to tell him everything?

"You know that girl I met on holiday?" I said. Jamie looked up.

"Charlie?" he said, looking interested.

"Yeah, Charlie," I said. "Remember her?"

"Sure do," Jamie said. "Nice legs, tight shorts . . ."

"Yeah, well, she's . . ." I almost said it but I couldn't.

"She's . . ." I said again. "She's going to . . ."

"Going to what?" Jamie said licking his fingers.

"Going to France," I said, saying the first thing that came into my head. "I had a letter from her," I added.

"Oh," said Jamie, looking a bit puzzled. "Why?"

"Why what?" I said.

"Why's she going to France?"

"Oh," I said. "I don't know."

"Didn't she say?" Jamie asked.

"No," I said, digging my fork into the cake. So much

132

for my attempt at soul-baring. Not many Rachel points there!

For some weird reason Mum mentioned Jamie's mum that night while we were eating.

"When's Jamie's mum's baby due?" she said.

"Baby?" said Rachel, staring at me, "*Jamie's mum*?"

"Yeah, she's pregnant," Mum said, spooning out lasagne.

"How did *you* know?" I said surprised.

"Saw her in Tescos," Mum said. "She's massive! She can't have long to go."

"Heavens! I bet that was a shock!" said Dad with a chuckle.

"Fancy having a baby at her age!" Rachel said. "She's even older than *you*, Mum!"

"Crikey! She must be almost prehistoric then!" said Mum sarcastically.

"Sorry, I didn't mean it like that," said Rachel, helping herself to salad. "But you were only twenty-two when you had *us*."

"And it was a shock for *me*, too," Mum said, biting into a carrot stick.

"Shock?" said Rachel, looking faintly horrified. "What? Weren't we planned?"

"Not *planned* exactly," Mum said. "But we were very pleased!"

Dad grinned at her across the table.

"Mum was still at college," Dad said. "And we had no money, so the timing wasn't great, but we managed. And you didn't turn out *too* bad!" Dad laughed. It didn't seem very funny to me.

"Babies don't always come at the most convenient times," Mum said. She grated pepper across her food with a vigorous twist of her wrist. Rachel was looking at me meaningfully across the table. I smelt a rat. Had she told Mum? Had she primed her to make a little speech about unplanned pregnancy? Why was everyone talking about babies? It was as if there was a big plot that everyone was in on except me. I ate my dinner in stony silence.

32

Rachel

Josh's friend Jamie's mum is having a baby. I bet it wasn't planned. Mum says we weren't planned either. Charming! That makes me feel great. Mum says babies are inconvenient. Well thanks Mum – sorry we spoiled your life! Josh says I must have told Mum about Charlie because it sounded like Mum was saying all that for *his* benefit. He said it was a fishy coincidence that everyone was talking about pregnancy all of a sudden. I said he was paranoid.

Josh was really angry. He stormed into my room accusing me of betraying him and not being trustworthy. (Those weren't the exact words he used – his were less polite.) He was furious about his calendar too. He's got this *Ride* calendar on the wall beside his bed with a box for every day of the month where you can write stuff. I went into his room with a marker pen and on May 29th I wrote BABY. Then I counted the weeks backwards and wrote 39 weeks, 38 weeks, 37 weeks etc.

"Why d'you have to mess with my stuff?" Josh said. "Just keep out of my room, all right!"

We ended up having a mega row. It wasn't the

calendar he was annoyed about. It was the fact that I won't let him forget he's about to become a father.

Charlie's thirty-five weeks now. There isn't long to go.

"How long are you going to go on pretending this baby doesn't exist, Josh?" I said. "Face facts!"

"I'd like to see you handle it any better!" Josh shouted. "You make it all sound so easy!"

"I know it's not easy," I said. "But you don't have to act like such a dickhead!"

Josh flipped when I said that.

"Get out of my room Rachel!" he shouted and he grabbed my shoulders and shoved me hard against the door frame.

"No!" I screamed, "I won't get out. And don't shove me!"

"Well don't call me a dickhead!" he said.

"Don't act like one then!" I said.

Josh was red in the face. I thought he was going to cry. But I beat him to it. I was weary of it all. Weary with trying to make him see sense, weary with keeping secrets, weary with being out of my depth. I sank on to the floor and burst into tears.

"I used to be so proud of you," I said. "I thought you were so wonderful. Everything you did, you did well. You were always up for it – up for anything."

Big tears splashed down my face. I sniffed loudly.

"But not any more" I said bitterly. "You've lost it Josh. You've lost your bottle."

I picked up a cushion off Josh's bed and wiped my face on it. Then I threw the damp cushion at Josh and walked out.

Mum came into my room a little while later. I still had a red puffy face. I was texting Nicola. Mum pushed a strand of hair behind my ear and looked at me thoughtfully.

"What's going on between you and Josh?" she said. I didn't answer.

"You used to be so close – such good mates. Now you seem to do nothing but argue and fight with each other."

"It's *him*," I said. "He's so . . ." I didn't finish the sentence.

"So what?" Mum said.

"Nothing," I said. "It's both of us. It's exam nerves. We're just both a bit uptight, that's all."

Mum looked unconvinced.

"Don't worry, Mum," I said, squeezing her hand. "It'll be all right."

Exam nerves! I wish!

33

Joshua

Jamie's mum had a baby girl. She's called Ella. She's got big eyes and no hair. I was at Jamie's house after we'd been playing basketball the other night. His mum was feeding her in front of the telly – no bottle or anything, just enormous pink boobs. Her nipples were the size of tennis balls. I didn't know where to look.

"She's cute isn't she?" Jamie said. I wasn't sure if he meant his mum or the baby so I nodded vaguely.

"She smells nice, too," Jamie said, "especially her head." Ella presumably. "And she smiles when I pick her up. She knows me already," he said. Definitely Ella.

Jamie's mum lifted the baby on to her shoulder. She did a surprisingly loud burp.

"Pardon me!" said Jamie's mum and we all laughed. Jamie went over and sat on the arm of his mum's chair.

"Can I hold her?" he said. She handed the baby to him. Jamie stood up, cradling her against his chest. He kissed the top of her head and rubbed his nose across her bald scalp. "Mmm!" he said. "Like velvet!" Then he pointed to her feet.

"Look at her toes," he said, "they're so dinky."

"Congratulations," I said. That seemed an appropriate thing to say.

"Thanks," said Jamie's mum, buttoning her shirt. She smiled at me. It was a very happy contented smile.

"She's magic isn't she?" Jamie said.

I nodded. The telly blared in the background.

"Do you want to hold her?" Jamie said. he was holding her out towards me like a parcel.

"No thanks," I said quickly. "I might drop her."

34

Rachel

Charlie wrote in early May. The letter was full of gruesome details.

She said she felt full to bursting and whenever she ate she got heartburn.

She said her breasts had gone all veiny like blue cheese.

She said her belly button had turned inside out and looked like the tied bit of a balloon (yuck!) and she'd had to take her stud out.

She said her tummy was *so* stretched she couldn't imagine wearing a crop top *ever* again! It was baggy T-shirts and disgusting stretchy trousers all the way now.

She said she couldn't sleep because she couldn't get comfy in bed and when she walked she got shooting pains down her legs.

She said when the baby rolled over it felt like someone was rearranging her organs!

I never knew pregnancy was so complicated. Men don't know they're born!

Charlie sounded very upbeat despite all this.

The baby's things are all ready she wrote.

I've got a Moses basket in my room and all his clothes in the drawer and stuff for doing his nappies. Mum says she'll help but she's not doing it *for* me. Fair enough.

I just wish it would hurry up and be born – it seems to have been such a long wait. Only three weeks to go now. I want my body back! I want to climb trees and jump in rivers again. Last summer seems a whole lifetime ago. I've been going swimming at the pool in town but it's not the same as Kettlebeck! They have an antenatal swimming class on Thursday afternoons. We all look like hippos! Most of the other women are *ancient* – all wrinkles and cellulite. At least my legs aren't that fat. And no varicose veins – thank God! And at least in the water you can't feel the baby's weight so you feel *almost* normal again. Anyway, only three weeks to go. Mind you, the nurse at the clinic says first babies are often late – up to a fortnight is pretty normal, she reckons.

Ten days late would be perfect. That would give me time to finish all my exams before giving birth. I'm revising pretty hard. I really want to do well. I suppose I want to prove myself – to show everyone who gave me a hard time and called me a slag. Maybe I want to do well for the baby too – so he can be proud of having a clever mum!

If the baby's born on time – or early – Mum's going to look after him and bring him into school so I can breastfeed him between exams. School have said I can sit my papers in a separate room from everyone else in case I need to go to the loo a lot. Apparently a chaperone will have to come with me to make sure I don't cheat, which should be fun!

Charlie didn't mention Josh. Maybe she's given up on him. Maybe she's run out of patience. Maybe she's written him out of the picture – an absentee dad. Who needs men anyway? I don't blame her. He still doesn't show any signs of getting in contact with her. Last time she wrote she said she was going to text him. I gave her his new mobile number but I don't know if she did. He didn't mention it. Not that he would. We hardly speak these days.

35

Rachel

In the middle of May it turned hot – just as we went on study leave. I did my revision sat in the back garden in a bikini and shades. Nicola came round too and we tested each other on stuff we'd revised. One day we tried speaking French all morning.

"What's French for six-pack?" said Nicola as Josh walked into the garden with his shirt off. She giggled.

This was a rare sighting of Josh. I think Nicola was disappointed he wasn't around more because she's madly in love with him – daft fool! But we hardly saw him. He *said* he was working at Jamie's house but I reckon they spent most of their time biking – or on Jamie's Playstation. In the past I would have tried encouraging Josh to work harder. I would have enjoyed being a good influence – not that Josh needed encouragement before. He's always done well at school (better than me in fact) because he's naturally clever and he's got what Dad calls "the gift of the gab". He's one of those annoying people who does well without any noticeable effort. But this time I *hoped* he'd come unstuck. I would be glad if he messed up his exams. That would teach him to be irresponsible and stupid!

I would have been glad about his accident too if it hadn't been so excruciatingly painful.

It was just before Spring Bank holiday. Mum was off work for a few days. She was gardening. I was lying on my bed reading *Romeo and Juliet* for the ninety-thousandth time.

I heard Jamie come into the garden and screech his bike brakes. He was shouting Mum's name.

"Mrs Graham! Mrs Graham!"

I looked out and saw Mum running across the lawn, pulling off her gardening gloves. She opened the front door and rummaged in the key drawer in the hall. Then she shouted up the stairs to me.

"Rachel! Joshua's had an accident. I'm going in the car."

"I'll come!" I said and I ran downstairs.

He wasn't far away. He was at the bottom of Smithies Field where they'd built their six-pack ramp. His bike was in a tangled heap against one of the mounds of earth they'd dug. Josh was lying on the ground on his side. He was white as a sheet and his face was contorted with pain.

"I'm sorry I left him," Jamie said. "I didn't know what to do. I didn't have my phone and Josh's is knackered." Josh's mobile was lying on the ground in bits. It looked like he'd landed on it as he fell. The ground was baked hard as concrete and there was a layer of brown dust all over Josh's clothes.

"Don't worry," said Mum calmly. "You did the right thing. You were right not to try and move him."

"He's says it hurts too much to move," Jamie said with a worried frown.

"Josh," said Mum touching his arm. "It's me, Mum. Can you tell me where it hurts?"

"Everywhere!" Josh said and he let out a howl of pain. His eyes were scrunched tightly shut. His chest was heaving.

"I can't breathe," he said in a panicky voice.

"We need to get you to hospital," Mum said. "Do you think you can stand?" Josh rolled over into a sitting position and opened his eyes. He looked terrible.

"Aaarh!" he yelled, clutching his shoulder. "It's agony!"

"Which is the worst pain?" Mum said patiently.

"My arm and my shoulder," he said, wailing. I reached out and took hold of his hand. His palm was grazed and gritty and there was a gash across his forehead that was oozing blood. It was his shoulder that looked the worst though. It looked all misshapen and his left arm was dangling limply. At the top of his chest, just above the neckline of his T-shirt there was a weird bulging lump.

Mum was wearing a big baggy shirt. She took it off and tied it across Josh's shoulder like a sling.

In the car on the way to the hospital Josh cried like a little kid. I haven't seen him cry like that for years. I sat beside him and held his hand.

"It kills," he said over and over. "Aaargh! It kills." I cried too. I always cry when Josh is hurt. It's a twins thing. Usually I do his crying for him.

It turned out to be a broken collarbone. Jamie said Josh had attempted a 360 – and *almost* done it. What was he trying to prove? That's what I want to know.

They don't do plastercasts for collarbones. They put him in one of those foamy slings to keep his arm rigid and sent him home with a big bottle of painkillers.

36

Joshua

I've had pain before – when I fell out of a tree and broke both my arms; when I hit my head on the garage wall; when Rachel trapped my finger in the bathroom door – but never like this. When my collarbone broke it felt as if someone had snapped me in half. My arm went like a puppet with its strings cut. And my chest hurt so much it felt like my lungs were caving in.

I was pretty mental to attempt a 360. I'd never done it before and the ground was like rock. Something Rachel said about me losing my bottle had really got to me. She said I wasn't up for it any more. That was like a red rag waved in a bull's face!

The approach to the ramp was my best yet. My new bike is sweet on dirt. I hit the lip perfect and used my legs and hips to swing the bike round. I had massive air and was already at 180. But as I was approaching 270 things started to go wrong. I was losing height and the back end had swiftly dropped. I could see the down ramp where I should have landed looming closer and closer. I knew I wasn't going to make it so I let go the bars and threw myself off the pedals, so I could roll free of the bike as I landed. (I had a bad fall a few months back and came crashing down on the bars. My ribs were bruised for weeks so I wasn't going to repeat that.) I hit the floor with a sickening crunch. I actually heard the bone crack. My phone was in my pocket. I felt it shatter as I hit the ground. And my bike was pretty mangled. The forks were badly bent. It'll cost me at least £100 to get it on the road again. What a pisser!

37

Rachel

Joshua's accident seemed to bring him to his senses a bit. He couldn't go anywhere or do anything so, for a week, he sat on a sun lounger in the back garden revising for his GCSEs. The sunny weather showed no sign of breaking. Weathermen were forecasting a drought summer. It was the hottest Spring Bank holiday for forty years.

As the week went on it got hotter and hotter. My tan was coming on well. I'd bought some coconut suntan oil – the same stuff Charlie had at Kettlebeck.

"D'you want some?" I said to Josh. (Things were almost back to normal between us again.) He was revising for Biology. The green exercise book had damp patches on the cover from his sweaty hands.

"Thanks," he said. "What do you call the outer layer of skin?"

"Epidermis," I said. "Shall I do your back – or will it be too sore?

"I'll do it," he said, leaning forward in the sun lounger. "What's the name of the pigment that filters out ultra-violet light?"

"Melanin," I said. "Here, you can't reach." I rubbed

some oil across Josh's shoulder blades taking care not to get any of it on the grey foamy strap of his sling. Josh flinched slightly.

"Does that hurt?" I said.

"No, it tickles," he said. He inhaled deeply and then he said, "Nice smell." I wondered if he recognized it. Did it remind him of Kettlebeck? And Charlie Lewis?

"It's a shame it wasn't your *right* arm," I said, looking at the sling holding Josh's left side in place. "You might have got out of doing your exams altogether!"

"No such luck," said Josh with a grin.

Mum came home from work at lunchtime and joined us in the garden. She made three tall drinks with chunks of ice and slices of lemon in them.

"Cheers, Mum," said Josh, raising his glass.

"Can I join the sun worshippers' club?" Mum said, hitching her skirt above her knees.

"No, it's exam slaves only," I said, winking at Josh.

"Oh poor things," Mum said. "Not long now. Then . . . FREEDOM!"

I didn't answer. Neither did Josh. I was thinking about Charlie. I don't know what Josh was thinking. Maybe he was thinking about her too because suddenly he said,

"What's today's date?"

"May 31st," said Mum. "Flaming June tomorrow."

* * *

I was still sipping my icy drink when the phone rang inside. Mum got up and went through the kitchen into the hallway. It was Charlie. I heard Mum say her name.

"Hello Charlie," Mum said. "How are you?" Mum was carrying the cordless phone out into the garden. "Will you be going to Kettlebeck again this summer?"

Charlie obviously gave a noncommittal reply because Mum said, "Oh well, maybe we'll see you some other time."

Mum was walking towards Josh. Josh looked as if he'd been injected with something to make him freeze. He was bolt upright and rigid on the sun lounger.

"Josh," said Mum brightly. "It's Charlie. She wants to speak to you."

Josh took the handset from her and cleared his throat. I could see his hand was shaking.

"Hullo," he said gruffly.

Mum sat back down in the deck chair and closed her eyes.

"That's a bolt from the blue," she said smiling. "He hasn't heard from her for months has he?"

"Mmmm," I said vaguely, sucking on a slice of lemon. I've been pretty discreet with Charlie's letters. The postman usually comes after Mum leaves for work. And my e-mail is password protected.

Mum obviously hadn't picked up anything.

I was watching Josh. On the other end of the line I could make out Charlie's voice but I couldn't catch what she was saying.

"Oh," said Josh, squirming with embarrassment. "Yeah . . . right . . ." He looked as if he wanted the patio to open up and swallow him whole.

"That's nice," he said feebly. Then he said, "Do you want to talk to Rachel now?" He thrust the handset at me.

"Hi!" I said, getting up from my chair. "I'll just take you inside, it's a bit hot out here in the garden."

Mum looked quizzically at Josh.

"How is she?" Mum said.

"Fine," said Josh, opening his Biology book again.

I took the phone into the living room where no one would overhear us.

"Have you had it?" I asked. "Tell me everything!"

Charlie was crying.

"I hate him!" she wailed. "I've gone through *all this* and given birth to a baby and all he can say is 'Oh, that's nice'! He's a thoughtless bastard!"

"He doesn't know what to say," I said, "and Mum was listening." Charlie was sobbing.

"I thought once I'd had it he'd want to come and see me, or at least talk to me. I thought he'd want to come and see his baby!" she howled.

"He will," I said. "Just give him time." There I was,

defending him again. How did I know what Josh might or might not do?

"How much time does he need?" Charlie said desperately. "He's had nine months!"

"I know," I said. I was trying to talk in a soothing voice. Charlie sounded in a bit of a state.

"Tell me about the baby," I said. She sniffed loudly.

"He's 3½kgs and he's fine," she said grumpily.

"How was the birth?" I said. Bad question.

"Bloody awful," said Charlie. "You can tell Josh *that*! It lasted ten hours and it hurt like hell. As if *he'd* care!"

"Don't be like that," I said.

"I was so naïve!" Charlie said angrily. "I thought he might *be* there. Who was I kidding? I thought he might just turn up, unannounced, and hold my hand and *be* with me. *I* didn't ask to have his baby!" Charlie shouted really loud when she said that. I held the phone away from my ear. She was crying again.

Trying to sound positive I said, "Is he nice?"

"Who?" Charlie said.

"The baby!" I said. "Dummy!"

"Yes," Charlie said. "He's *gorgeous*!" She sounded as if she was laughing and crying at the same time.

"Have you decided what to call him?" I said.

"Yes," she said, "Sam."

I didn't answer.

"Are you still there?" Charlie said.

"Yeah," I said. "Why?"

"Why what?"

"Why Sam?"

"I just like the name," she said. "Short and sweet. And we had a cat called Sam when I was little – not that the baby looks like a cat or anything – but he was a nice cat!" She laughed a bit hysterically.

"Did you tell Josh?" I said.

"Tell him what?" she said.

"That you'd called the baby Sam?" I said.

"Of course," she said. "Why?"

38

Rachel

I sent Charlie a card and some Pooh Bear socks for the baby. It seemed rather a feeble gesture when what she really wanted was my brother but I reckoned it was better than nothing.

Josh was moody and silent for the next few days. He stayed in his room a lot, lying on his bed and listening to loud music. When Mum asked him why he wasn't revising he said he couldn't concentrate because his arm hurt so much. I said nothing to him. He was like a bomb waiting to go off.

The night before our first Maths paper the weather broke and there was an almighty thunderstorm. Rain pounded against the windows and the garden steamed like a tropical forest.

The next morning I got up and Mum and Dad went off to work as usual. I had a shower and ate some breakfast. Our exam started at ten o'clock. By nine there was no sign of Josh so I knocked on his door. He didn't answer. I knocked again. Still he didn't answer. So I went in. Josh had the covers over his head. Under the sheets I could see his shoulders shaking as if he was laughing and there was a muffled sound like someone suppressing a fit of the giggles. I thought he was about to play a joke on me – spring out or roar or something – so I pre-empted him and made a grab for the covers. I whisked the duvet off like a magician swiping a tablecloth from under the cups and saucers.

But Josh wasn't laughing. He was crying. He was curled up small and he was sobbing like a baby.

"Josh, what's the matter?" I said, horrified.

"Go away please," he said in a tiny thin voice.

"You've got to get up," I said. "We've got Maths. The exam starts in under an hour."

"I'm not going," Josh said.

"What d'you mean?" I said.

"I can't do it," he sobbed. "I can't cope!"

"Josh, you *can* cope," I said. "You're brilliant at Maths."

"I had a dream," he said, "about Sam."

"Charlie's baby?" I said. I still had Josh's duvet in my hand.

"No," Josh said. "*Our* Sam. Little Sam." He wasn't looking at me.

"Little Sam," I said, remembering. "You always called him that."

"He was in the car in his kids' seat," Josh continued. "He was holding a painting of a horse he'd done at nursery. Remember how he liked horses? There was one in the field behind Tesco that we used to go and feed. And we had a game – me and him. He used to sit on my back and say 'Giddy-up!' and I'd pretend to gallop." I nodded. I did remember that, now Josh mentioned it. I dropped the duvet on to the bed. Josh was face down on the bed, burying his head in the pillow. Slowly he sat up, clasping the pillow in front of him.

"Mum was driving," he continued. "In the dream she was talking to Sam. She wasn't concentrating. Suddenly a car was coming, coming straight at them. Sam saw it through the window. It was a red car. It smashed into the side of our car – into Sam. Sam was screaming. I could hear him screaming Rach! And Mum was slumped across the wheel, bleeding. Then I woke up." Josh squeezed the pillow and sobbed. "She's only called the baby Sam to get back at me!" he said, punching the pillow fiercely. He punched it so hard he hurt his arm. "Ow! Bugger!" he said, clutching his sore shoulder.

"Careful," I said.

I sat down on the bed. It was damp with sweat – or tears – or both.

"Charlie didn't know our brother was called Sam," I said calmly. "She named him after her cat!"

Josh looked incredulous.

"What did you say?" he said. He wiped his face on the sheets.

"Her cat," I said, pulling a face. "She had a cat called Sam when she was little."

Josh didn't answer. Then he said, "As if?" He almost smiled. "Are you *sure* she didn't know?" he said.

"I'm sure," I said. "She just liked the name."

There was a pause then Josh said, "Why did I dream about him, Rach?" He let the pillow fall on to the bed. "I've never dreamt about him before. Never."

"You've got a lot of stuff in your head right now," I said.

Josh flopped back on to the mattress. He looked exhausted.

"I thought I'd forgotten him," he said. "But it still hurts – I really miss him."

"I miss him, too," I said. Josh sat up and I gave him a hug. He started crying again.

"You never cried when Sam died," I said.

"Well, I'm making up for it now," Josh said. We sat there for a few minutes. Just crying and hugging each other. Then, over Josh's shoulder, I saw the clock.

"Come on," I said, handing him a tissue. "You've got an exam in half an hour."

39

Joshua

What I said when Charlie phoned was so deeply naff. I bet I sounded a right idiot! But what was I supposed to say, with Mum listening? How big is he? How was labour? Does he look like me? Does he look like Little Sam?

Since she phoned I can't stop thinking about her. About her, and Sam. What's he like? Has he got big eyes like Jamie's baby sister? What *colour* are his eyes? Has he got hair? And Charlie? Is she OK? Does *she* look different? Is she breastfeeding him like Jamie's mum? Is she happy? It's so hard to picture them both.

When she phoned and I heard her voice it seemed real for the first time. It made me wish I'd phoned her months ago instead of being such a chicken. Rachel kept saying I was being selfish and that I didn't care. Maybe she was right – partly. But it wasn't as simple as that. For a start I was scared Charlie would hate me for getting her pregnant in the first place. I was so mad with myself I suppose I tried to blank it all out, to pretend it wasn't happening. What does Rachel call it? Denial.

But even if I'd phoned Charlie, or written to her, or even gone to see her, what was I supposed to *say*?

Hi! Sorry I made you pregnant! Sorry I messed up your life!

It wasn't like *I* could have the baby instead of her or anything. It was inside her body not mine. I couldn't change that.

At first I hoped she'd have an abortion so the problem would go away. If it was me I'd probably have done that – got rid of it when it still looked like those tadpoley things in Rachel's book.

I never really doubted that it was mine. Charlie told me I was the only person she'd slept with. I believe her. She's got more balls than me.

Rachel kept reminding me I was about to be a father – as if I was likely to forget. The word "father" scares the life out of me. How can I be a father at sixteen, seventy miles away from a girl I hardly know and a baby I've never seen?

My collarbone was mended by the middle of June. I went to hospital the day before my last exam and they took the cuff and collar thing off a week early. "Good healing bones," the nurse said. My arm felt all floaty and light. Dad challenged me to a game of pool to celebrate. We've got a pool table up in the attic. Dad and I have an ongoing tournament – we play a frame most nights when he comes in from work. I usually win. When I had my accident I was leading the series by 18 frames to 3. Dad racked the balls up and broke. He potted a yellow straight away.

"Jammy!" I said. He potted another.

"Oh yes!" he said, punching the air. Then he missed and it was my turn. I was rubbish. Five weeks in a sling had left my arm all stiff and useless. I missed all the reds and gave Dad an extra shot. He potted three yellows in a row.

"They call me mell-ow yell-ow . . ." he started singing, jigging about with his cue. He always sings that when he pots a yellow. It's some sad Sixties song I think. At last I sank a red.

"Can Joshua Graham recover his lost form?" Dad said in a hushed commentator's voice. I grinned. I took a shot and potted another red. Dad gasped dramatically. Then I fouled the white ball by mistake.

"Not today," said Dad, answering his own question. There were only two of Dad's balls left on the table. He potted them both in quick succession.

"Nice balls," I said. Dad pulled a camp face. Then, with a very flukey shot, he potted the black.

"18–4!" Dad said. "It's a comeback!" I laughed.

"How were your exams?" Dad said.

"OK," I said. Actually they were awful. I could only answer half the questions in History because I hadn't done enough revision and English Lit was really hard.

"How about the hospital?" Dad said. "Is everything healed up?"

"I think so," I said. "They took an X-ray and everything looked OK. The nurse said I had good healing bones." I circled my left arm stiffly. "It doesn't hurt any more."

"No more stunts for a while then, eh?" He ruffled my hair. Then he gave me a big hug. He's hugged me a lot lately. Maybe he knows there's something wrong. Perhaps he can tell instinctively. Maybe it's a father-son thing. Father. Son. It's slowly sinking in that I'm a father. I've got a son.

I've thought about Dad a lot in the last few months. I reckon he's a pretty good dad. He's so positive and he's always there when I need him. The other day I remembered something that happened years ago. I was playing in the sea, jumping on and off a rock at the water's edge. The tide was coming in. My feet were getting wetter and wetter. Suddenly a huge wave came. I was standing on the rock and swirly water surrounded me – deep water, too deep to stand up in. I was frightened and I shouted for Dad. Dad waded out in his clothes. The water was up to his waist. He lifted me off the rock and carried me back to the beach. Even now I can remember the feel of his strong arms and the smell of his salty skin and his warm breath on my face. I remembered that when

I was in the bath the other night. It just came back to me like a warm breeze. It made me cry. I'm not sure why.

If I'm going to be a father I want to be a father like Dad. Not some stupid kid who falls off his bike all the time. I want to be a decent dad, a proper dad, the sort of dad a kid is proud of. The sort of dad who rescues you out of the sea.

40

Rachel

Our last exam was a Thursday. At the end of it everyone was demob happy. Danny Shaw let a fire extinguisher off outside the gym and there was foam all over the corridor.

"Foam party!" shouted Jamie, diving into it. A gang of us caught the bus into town and went to a pub called Shady's. They must have known we were all underage but they served us anyway. Some of Josh's friends got really hammered. A load of them jumped in the fountain in front of Marks and Spencer's and Jamie pulled a moonie at some people in a taxi. Mark Benson was sick outside MacDonald's.

"Would you like regular fries with that or large?" said Danny Shaw.

Joshua was uncharacteristically quiet.

"Here, Josh," said Danny when we reached the park, "I dare you to put your boxers on top of the bandstand!"

"Nah," said Josh. "I'm not in the mood."

"Lighten up Josh," said Jamie. "They're over. You're a free man! Today is the first day of the rest of your life." Jamie grinned a drunken smile.

"That's a bit deep for you isn't it Jamie?" Nicola said. Jamie had his arm round her. He started kissing her ear lobe. Nicola must have decided Jamie's a better prospect than Josh – or else she was too drunk to care.

Josh looked miserable. I was hungry and it was getting late.

"Shall we go?" I said. Josh looked grateful for the excuse.

We caught a bus home – just me and Josh.

"Are you OK?" I said.

"Kind of," said Josh. The bus pulled away from the park. I could see Danny Shaw climbing on the iron railings. Jamie had found a traffic cone and was wearing it on his head. Josh shook his head when he saw them.

"Daft buggers," he said. He sounded weary.

We rode along in silence, then I said, "Penny for your thoughts?"

"I thought you always knew what I was thinking without me telling you," Josh said dryly.

"Not any more," I said. "You've lost me lately." Josh was staring out of the window.

"Thanks for writing to Charlie," he said. I was taken by surprise.

"I thought you thought I was a nosy cow," I said.

"Nosy bitch wasn't it?" he said.

"Worse still!" I said.

"Sorry," Josh said. Then he said suddenly,

"I want to go and see her – see *them*." I looked at him to check he wasn't joking.

"Seriously?" I said. He nodded.

"Do you think she'll want to see me?" Josh said. He looked all boyish and vulnerable.

"She might," I said, raising my eyebrows. "She'll probably be glad of the opportunity to slap your face." I grinned and Josh half-grinned back.

"I can take it!" he said. He said it like a cartoon action hero. I thought of Charlie's gran in her rhinestone boots. And her man-hating mum. Maybe they'd all line up and hit him!

"I think I want to tell Mum and Dad too," he said. "How do you think they'll take it?"

"I think they'll kill you," I said.

"I can take that too," said Josh with a gulp. He looked at me. The bus was turning into our road. An ice-cream van went by playing *Singing in the Rain*.

"You're a mate, Rach," Josh said. I linked my little finger on to his, like we used to when we were kids and we had a secret.

"Twins," I whispered. Josh smiled.

41

Rachel

Mum had cooked a special meal to celebrate the end of exams. They'd even opened a bottle of champagne that had been in the fridge since Christmas.

Dad was singing "School's out for sum-mer . . .!" as he served the roast potatoes. "Alice Cooper," he said," I went to see him when I was your age. He had a snake on stage – wrapped round his neck – and lots of fake blood."

"Yuck!" I said. "And you say Eminem is sick!" Dad winked at me.

"Nothing new under the sun," he said.

Josh was chewing his food silently. He looked tense. I wondered at what point in the meal he was planning to tell them.

"Have a drink, Josh," said Dad filling his glass.

"Jamie was pretty tanked up wasn't he?" I said to Josh.

"Oh dear, was he?" Mum said. I told her about the traffic cone and Danny's foam party.

"Twas ever thus," said Dad with a sage nod.

"I half expected you to come home with your pants on your head," Mum said to Josh.

"Danny dared him to put his pants on top of the bandstand," I said, "but he was very sensible and refused." Mum smiled.

"Party pooper!" said Dad, sloshing champagne into his glass.

Josh said nothing about Charlie all through the first course. Mum offered him seconds of chicken and roasties but he said no.

"I'm not actually feeling all that hungry," he said. I was watching him like a hawk. It looked as if chewing every mouthful was an effort.

Mum cleared the plates away and brought in a big bowl of strawberries.

"I hope you've got room for *these*!" she said. I love strawberries. I ate two bowls full.

When we'd finished Dad topped-up the glasses and cleared his throat. Pushing his chair back from the table he stood up and raised his glass. "I'd like to propose a toast to our lovely twins, Rachel and Joshua," he said. Mum raised her glass too and beamed at us.

"To a glorious future!"

"A glorious future!" repeated Mum.

I looked at Josh across the table. Now was the moment. Just do it Josh. Josh looked as if he was about to be sick. I eyeballed him – willing him to speak.

"Talking of the future," Josh said tentatively. "I've got some news."

Dad was pouring another glass of champagne. He leaned across the table to pour one for Mum.

"I think you'd better sit down, Dad," I said quietly. Mum looked worried.

"Is everything all right?" she asked.

"Kind of," said Josh. Then he said, "Well actually, no, not really . . ." he was staring at his empty bowl. Trickles of cream mingled with a pool of strawberry juice, making pink swirls.

"It's Charlie," Josh said. Dad looked up from his strawberries and grinned.

"Charlie from Kettlebeck, with the nice legs?" he said.

"How many other Charlies do we know?" I said snappily.

"All right," said Dad. "Keep your hair on. I was just checking."

"She phoned just last week," Mum said, looking at Dad. "Out of the blue."

Mum looked at Josh. He looked grave.

"Has something happened to her Joshua?" Mum said.

Josh opened his mouth.

"She's . . ." he said. Then he hesitated. I looked encouragingly at him.

"She's . . . pregnant. Or rather she *was* pregnant.

She's had a baby. That was why she phoned." There was an awful silence. Dad wasn't grinning any more.

"God!" said Mum after a pause.

"She didn't phone out of the blue," I said. "I've been writing to her since the summer."

"So you already *knew*?" Mum said.

"Yes," I said.

"Both of you knew?" Mum said, staring at Josh.

"Yes," Josh said.

"Since when?" Mum said.

"Since she first found out," I said. "Octoberish."

"Hence the books about pregnancy," said Mum, "and all the questions." I nodded.

"So you've known *all this time* and you've only just seen fit to tell us!" Mum snatched the napkin off her knee and scrumpling it into a ball she dropped it on the table.

Dad was still struggling to get the plot.

"Hang on a minute," Dad said. "This baby? She not saying it's *yours*, is she, Josh?"

Dad's face had clouded over now. I wondered if he was about to shout. Dad hardly ever shouts but when he does he makes the house shake.

"It *is* mine," Josh said.

"So she says!" said Mum, pushing her chair back from the table.

"Mum!" I said indignantly.

"I'm sure it is," said Josh.

Dad slammed his spoon down on the tablecloth.

"Don't be stupid!" he said. "You only went out with her for five minutes and you haven't seen her since. How can it be yours?"

"Dad!" Josh shouted. "I know what I did all right! I had sex with her and it's my baby!"

"Don't shout at *me*!" Dad said, glaring at Josh. "*When* did you have sex with her?"

"That's none of your business, Dad," I said. Then he was glaring at *me*.

"So it's none of my business that my sixteen year-old son has banged up some slapper at a campsite!" said Dad, his face going red.

"Don't make it sound so smutty, Dad," I said.

"Well what was it?" he barked. "True undying love!? At fifteen? *Romeo and Juliet*? It wasn't just smutty! It was illegal!"

Josh stood up, knocking his chair flying, and stormed towards the door.

"Don't you DARE walk out!" Dad roared, banging his fist on the table. Josh froze.

"So let's get this straight," Dad yelled. "My only son who's barely turned sixteen is telling me that he's a father, is that right?" Josh stood still, staring at his feet. "What a bloody mess!" Dad shouted. "What a bloody stupid God-awful mess!"

"Brian," Mum said. "Calm down. Shouting won't help the situation."

"So what are we supposed to do, Sheila?" Dad said, rounding on Mum. "Pour another glass of champagne and toast the glorious future!"

"Let's try and talk about it," Mum said. She stroked Dad's arm and he relaxed a little.

Josh sat back down and fiddled with his tablemat. I tried to catch his eye but he wouldn't look at me.

"Why didn't you tell us sooner?" Mum said. "Then we could have *done* something."

"Done what?" I said fiercely. "Persuaded Charlie to have an abortion?"

"I didn't *say* that," Mum said.

"Well what then?" I said.

Dad sat back in his chair and sighed heavily.

"What are two sixteen year-olds supposed to do with a baby?" he said. He was still red in the face. Beads of sweat had appeared all round the edge of his hair. "How are you supposed to bring it up? You're still kids yourselves! You've got your whole life in front of you. And what about your education? You're still at school! *Charlie's* still at school! She doesn't want a *baby*! For heaven's sake! It's like dogs – babies aren't just for Christmas, they're for *life*!"

"Babies *aren't* convenient," I said crossly. "*You* said *that*, Mum!"

"Did I?" Mum said.

"Yes," said Josh. "You did. I thought you *knew* when you said that."

172

"How was I supposed to *know*?" Mum said. "I'm not telepathic!"

Josh glanced at me across the table and I knew he was sorry he hadn't trusted me. Mum sighed.

"What are we supposed to say?" she said, looking at me and shrugging. "What did you *think* we'd say?" I didn't answer.

"So what happens next?" Mum said. "What were you planning on doing?"

"I dunno," Josh mumbled, poking a teaspoon into the edge of his mat.

"How's Charlie?" Mum said. "How's she coping?"

"I don't really know," Josh said. "She hasn't said."

I nearly told Mum Josh had only spoken to her the once but I didn't want them to start shouting at him again so I said, "She had a long labour. It lasted ten hours, she said."

"Ten hours isn't bad for a first baby," Mum said.

"Ten hours?" said Josh incredulously. "Is that how long it took?"

"It doesn't take five minutes like in the movies you know Josh," Mum said. "Real life isn't like that." She was fiddling with the locket round her neck. "Presumably her mum knows?" she said. I could tell she was hurt we hadn't told her.

"Yes," I said. "She's known since about five months. She wanted Charlie to have an abortion too."

"I bet she's delighted with *you*," Mum said, looking at Josh.

"It wasn't just *his* fault," I said. Josh was biting his lip.

"So who's fault was it then?" Dad said cynically.

"Both of them," I said quietly.

There was a silence when no one said anything. Then Josh said, "It's a boy – the baby – it's a boy and she's called him . . ." Josh's voice cracked as he said it, ". . . Sam."

When he said Sam's name Josh started crying – not just wet eyes, but really crying, with loud sobs. He picked up his napkin and buried his face in it. Mum and Dad looked awkward. It's so rare for Josh to cry. I don't think they were expecting it.

Mum softened a little.

"Oh Josh," she said more sympathetically.

"Sorry," Josh said, through his sobs. Mum got up from her chair and went to put her arms around him. Josh turned his face towards her and sobbed.

"I'm really sorry," he said again.

I looked at Dad. The anger had drained out of his face now and he just looked sad. He got up and walked towards the window where he stood looking out at the garden. I went up behind him and hugged him round his waist.

"It'll be okay," I said. "Everything will work out all right." Dad didn't answer. Josh was blowing his nose on the napkin. Mum pulled away and ran her hand through her hair.

"Some glorious future," Josh said with a sniff. "What a cock-up."

"Perhaps not the best choice of phrase," Mum said with half a smile. Then suddenly she said "My God! I'm a granny and I'm only thirty-eight!"

"Sorry," said Josh again.

"I think I need a drink," Mum said, sitting back down at the table and pouring herself some more champagne.

"Josh," she said, offering the bottle to Josh.

"No thanks," Josh said. "I don't really feel like celebrating."

"Brian?" Mum said. "Will you have the last drop?" Dad turned round. As he approached the table I saw that he had been crying too. He sat down without speaking. Mum filled his glass.

"I think I need to rewrite my speech," Dad said in a subdued voice, looking at Josh.

Josh opened his mouth to apologise again but Dad cut him off.

"Don't say sorry again Josh," he said holding up his hand. "I know you're sorry." Josh and Dad looked at each other.

There was a pause, then Mum spoke quietly, raising her glass, "To the future," she said, "and whatever it holds. And to Sam."

Epilogue

So here we are, in the car, in Doncaster. It took an hour-and-a-half to drive here – Dad got lost finding the street.

Josh looks great. Mum bought him a new T-shirt. It's purple – Charlie's favourite colour. And he's got the friendship bracelet back on his wrist. I had to mend it for him because he'd cut it in half.

We all went to Mothercare and bought Sam a babygrow with hedgehogs on it. Mum wrapped it in silver paper.

I don't know what Josh is planning to do long term – I don't think he knows either – but he wanted to come and see Charlie and the baby and Mum and Dad said they'd bring him – which is pretty nice of them, considering. I don't know what Charlie said when Josh phoned to ask if we could come. I didn't ask. It's between *them* now. Whatever she said he looked pretty happy about it.

Dad stops the car.

"Are you sure this is the right house?" Mum says.

"Yeah" I say, "number forty-six. Charlie said it

had a blue door." At Number 46 there is no sign of life. At the downstairs window there are net curtains.

"I hope she's in after we've come all this way," Dad says, switching off the engine.

"She's expecting us," Josh says, unfastening his seat belt. He looks very nervous.

"You go," Mum says. "We'll stay in the car." She pats his hand gently.

"Are you sure?" Josh says.

"Sure," says Mum.

"Thanks," says Josh with a grateful smile. He lifts the silver package off the back seat.

"All the best, Josh," Dad says.

"Up for it?" I ask.

"Up for it," Josh says quietly. I wink at him.

Josh opens the car door and steps out onto the pavement. Tucking the shiny silver parcel under his arm he closes the door, smiling nervously at us.

"Go for it!" I whisper. Josh opens the gate and walks slowly towards the house holding the parcel against his chest. He passes a bush with purple flowers and a plastic garden seat. There is a football on the path. Josh kicks it onto the lawn. When he reaches the front door he looks back over his shoulder anxiously and, peering through the car windows, we give him the thumbs up.

"Bless him," says Mum as he reaches for the doorbell.

Charlie opens the door. She looks pretty much like she did last time we saw her at Kettlebeck. Same fantastic blonde hair. Same great legs. But she looks older, more cautious. She is holding Sam, expertly supporting him over her shoulder.

"Has he got hair?" Mum says, squinting past me.

"I can't see," I say.

For a moment Josh and Charlie stand looking stiffly at each other. Charlie looks frosty. I wonder if Josh is apologising. He's staring at his feet.

"She must be so mad with him," I say.

"She hasn't hit him yet," Dad says. "That's a relief!"

Then he says, "Wind the window down Sheila, so I can hear what they're saying!"

"No!" says Mum. "I will not!" Mum slaps Dad affectionately and Dad laughs. As he laughs Josh reaches out and gives Charlie the silver parcel.

Charlie takes it and holds on to it for a while. They are looking at each other. Josh says something to her and for the first time Charlie smiles. Then she lifts the baby down off her shoulder and gives him to Josh. Hesitantly Josh takes his son in his arms and cradles him against his chest. Out of the corner of my eye I see Mum blink away tears. I squeeze her hand as Josh lowers his chin and kisses the baby on the top of his head.

"Sam", I whisper under my breath. "Baby Sam."

A note from the author

As someone who is
scared by the tamest of
rollercoasters – but as the mother
of three sons whose physical daring
simultaneously thrills and terrifies me –. I
enjoyed creating Josh. I love the energy with
which he approaches life.
Like his sister Rachel I am both exhilarated and
exasperated by him. Finding himself way out of his
depth, Josh's response is to run, but I love him
no less for it! Hopefully, in time, he will throw
himself into parenthood as whole-heartedly as he
does everything else.

Sue Mayfield is the author of BLUE as well
as I CARRIED YOU ON EAGLES' WINGS and
HANDS IN CONTRARY MOTION

BLUE

Sue Mayfield

'You've lost weight . . . Mind you don't get anorexic,'
Hayley said, sounding concerned. 'You're all skin and
bone!' She glanced sideways at Ruth Smith, and they
smiled conspiratorially.

'Anna-rexic!' said Ruth with a snort of laughter . . .

When Hayley, the most popular girl at school,
wants to be her best mate, new girl Anna
Goldsmith can't believe her luck. Charismatic
and confident, Hayley Parkin is definitely
someone to be in with – who *wouldn't* want to be
her friend?!

But this friendship comes at a price. Because
Hayley enjoys playing games. Spiteful, vicious
and dangerous games . . .

MAGENTA ORANGE

Echo Freer

Magenta Orange has the world at her feet. If she could just stop tripping over them . . .

Bright, sassy and massively accident-prone, Magenta is seen as a bit of a jinx by her mates – and a positive disaster-zone by the boy of her dreams!

Blind to the longing looks of her best friend, Daniel, oblivious to the sweet-nothings of the school geek, Spud, Magenta has set her sights on Year Eleven babe-magnet, Adam Jordan.

And she will risk anything, even total public humiliation, in her relentless pursuit of a date . . .

ORDER FORM

Also available in the 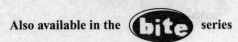 series

0 340 81732 1	Nostradamus and Instant Noodles *John Larkin*	£4.99	❏
0 340 81746 1	Festival *David Belbin*	£4.99	❏
0 340 81762 3	Speak *Laurie Halse Anderson*	£4.99	❏
0 340 80519 6	Blue *Sue Mayfield*	£4.99	❏
0 340 84148 6	Magenta Orange *Echo Freer*	£4.99	❏
0 340 80520 X	Four Days Till Friday *Pat Moon*	£4.99	❏

All Hodder Children's books are available at your local bookshop, or can be ordered direct from the publisher. Just tick the titles you would like and complete the details below. Prices and availability are subject to change without prior notice.

Please enclose a cheque or postal order made payable to *Bookpoint Ltd*, and send to: Hodder Children's Books, 130 Milton Park, Abingdon, OXON OX14 4SB, UK. Email Address: orders@bookpoint.co.uk

If you would prefer to pay by credit card, our call centre team would be delighted to take your order by telephone. Our direct line *01235 400414* (lines open 9.00 am–6.00 pm Monday to Saturday, 24 hour message answering service). Alternatively you can send a fax on *01235 400454*.

TITLE		FIRST NAME		SURNAME	

ADDRESS	

DAYTIME TEL:		POST CODE	

If you would prefer to pay by credit card, please complete:
Please debit my Visa/Access/Diner's Card/American Express (delete as applicable) card no:

Signature .... Expiry Date: ....

If you would NOT like to receive further information on our products please tick the box. ❏